Money Problems

a story collection

Cameron Davis

CONTENTS

In dedicated memory of Ethel Cole,
Forever my grandmother

YOUNG & DUMB

WOMEN MADE CALCULUS

—

Carson and Nadia left the movies as soon as it ended. When the credits began to roll down the Theater screen, they were the first ones at the door exit, hand in hand, walking in stride. Earlier they had dined at Brady's, a three star restaurant. From there they went to see *Landings of Doom*, a romance, and with the movie theater full, they cuddled throughout the whole film.

They reached Carson's car and he opened the door for Nadia. Then he cranked the engine up and drove out of the parking lot.

"Nice movie," Carson said. "Could have been better though. The drive-in theater ending was clever. Imagine the making-out couples did in those."

"They shut those drive-in theaters down because guys were getting the wrong impression on girls," said Nadia, seduction in her tone. "Don't flex like you were watching that movie."

Carson swerved his 97' Nissan Maxima onto Fowler Avenue, the main road to the University of South Florida. The sky grew darker by the minute. The Maxima read 10:30 on the dash as it accelerated into the night. "I was just saying I've seen better movies."

"Likewise. But don't act like you did something you didn't and didn't do something you did. Be real with yours,

Carly boy."

"What?" Carson was confused. "And how many times have I told you my name isn't *Carly*?"

Carson had one hand on the wheel, and the other hand on his girlfriend thigh. A traffic light ahead turned red but the V6 Nissan kept going. He ran the light!

Carson was in quite the hurry to get back to the dormitory. He had a big Calculus exam tomorrow and wanted to cram in some last minute studying. Of course "last minute" in the college world meant a two hour study session even though he had to wake up at seven a.m. to get ready for class.

"You know, I have class tomorrow too, but you don't see me running myself mad over school," said Nadia. "Do you?"

Nadia was a special kind of beauty. She had blonde hair, a perfect sized body, and a cute face. Her beauty was celestial. You had to see her to believe it.

"Sweetheart we both have school in the morning but I have an exam that will prove a whole lot. We're talking about my future here and maybe even my stint at USF."

"If you say so," she said. And with that, she sunk lower in the passenger seat.

Easily over the speed limit, Carson completed a couple turns and then turned onto Nadia's dormitory street. He parked the car then cut the engine, quickly rounding the car to open Nadia's passenger door. Again, it was time to push Nadia's buttons to see how far she would take it. Desperately, Carson had been investing a lot of effort into Nadia. And there was only one way Nadia could pay him off. Carson wanted to get laid!

"You good for tomorrow?" Carson asked. "You

know I love you, don't you?"

Nadia unbuckled herself and swerved around in her seat to face Carson.

Carson figured it was his job to push Nadia's buttons to test how far she'd go. After all, Carson was a junior in college in which he had yet to ice some college trim. He wanted to see how far she would dive tonight.

Nadia sucked her teeth. "Not now Carson. It's too dark out to see in the first place. Besides it's 11:00 and we have class tomorrow. Not to mention your life or death test. It's close to curfew too, you know?"

———

"Curfew!" She reminded him! It had almost slipped his mind. Carson had planned on being on the brink of curfew earlier but now things seemed different. The test of his life was coming up in less than eight hours and he needed to prepare.

"Hot chili peppers you're right!" Carson said. Putting his arm around Nadia, he held her while she stood outside his car. He had curfew to make but this was still another opportunity at Nadia.

"So what's with us?"

"Carl I'm sorry, but not tonight okay. Its late and I don't have time for this." She shoved her way passed him and then walked across the lawn to her dormitory.

Carson watched Nadia's voluptuous legs stagger away like an angler watching a fish jump off a line. Carson was thinking whether or not he should run and grab her and yell, "Well Then: When The FUCK ARE WE?"

He decided not to, and watched her go instead. *Witch,*

he thought.

"Nadia you just gone leave like that? I'm not even worth a kiss goodbye?"

As the blonde was bending the corner, she waved over at Carson and said, "Goodbye, Carly boy." A Blackberry cellular phone flashed on in her hand.

The ever-so-protective boyfriend waited until the dorm security door closed.

Next time, he'd show her he wasn't playing. Carson was going to start murdering these college women. Ted Bundy Time.

He got back in the car and shot up Holly Street to Beta, his dormitory building. Distance to distance, it took him six minutes to get to his dorm from Nadia's. He parked his car and got out. Carson knelt and saw it was dry underneath his Maxima. Dodging the car mechanics, he had changed his oil before taking Nadia out. So far, so good.

The Maxima read 11:10 pm. He didn't see a prehistoric Ford Shelby anywhere, which was a good sign for him because he had limited time to study.

Battered and raggedy, the twenty two year old Ford Shelby belonged to Carson's roommate, Andy.

Andy was a hockey athlete at the university and since there was no funding for the hockey team, the Housing Committee had randomly paired each hockey player with an Engineer major. Unfortunately for Carson, his name had been picked.

After checking to make sure his car doors were locked, Carson went into the dorm, down the hallways, and into the kitchen to grab two slices of leftover pizza from the fridge. He warmed them in the microwave and began to eat without a beverage to spare.

A tall, gangly scholar of some ilk suddenly entered and grabbed a two liter soda out of the fridge. He said, "Hey, Carl."

"What's good, Sid?"

It was not unusual to find students still awake past eleven o'clock. In the frenzy of an exam, students would abuse coffee, caffeine, or anything powerful enough to stay awake.

"Everything is everything. Say, Andy isn't around huh?" Sid asked. "Wish it could stay that way."

Then Sid left. Tiny jeans crippled his gait as he staggered off. Sid's motto was: "Do you." It's the new style. You should wonder what his closet looked like.

Carson knew Sid since freshmen year. He was a double Engineer major just like Carson. Sid was a metro sexual from Connecticut, which was fine on Carl's end. But Sid was attacked by Andy ever since he came to the house their sophomore years.

Andy was a senior.

Carson quickly finished his pizza, downed a cup of tap water and off he went to his room. A bunk bed and a big mirror on the wall were the only pieces of furniture in the room. Junk and clutter was everywhere.

His roommate sister lived in the area, somewhere in St. Petersburg across the bridge, and offered them to do there laundry at her place. Carson would take her up on this offer ASAP to help FEMA this Hurricane.

Carson rummaged and gratefully found his laptop. He quickly searched his USF G-mail account for any new e-mail. Like maybe his Calculus professor had postponed the exam.

He hadn't. Turning the computer off, Carson placed it over a stack of books, put his Calculus binders on a desk by the bunker, and hopped in the shower.

He quickly hopped out and opened his Math materials and buried his mind into limits, slopes, logarithms, all in the likes of Calculus. Calculus was so time consuming that he had taken his bath and ate so all he'd have to do was sleep whenever his body finally dozed off for good.

As his mind began to fade, Carson noticed some envelopes on the floor underneath the thin door spacing that was barely high enough for the envelopes to fit through. He cracked the door open and picked up the pieces of mail documents and read them. They each were for Andy and someone had opened one of them. They were dirty and ripped with shoe marks on them.

Carson hadn't seen them before. He shook and blew the envelopes, then placed them on the top bunk, where Andy slept.

Carson sat down and was about to divulge in another round of Killer Calculus when he heard loud shouts and screams from outside. Carson looked up toward the alarm clock and it read 12:15 in a dazed green.

Andy had arrived. And his fellow party animals had followed him home.

The door was half open when Andy, drunk as a skunk, almost knocked the door off its hinges. He galloped inside the room, holding a beer in his right hand, leaning on the door with his left.

"Casey?" he liked to call his roommate. "You still up? Trust me, you won't believe what happened tonight at the grad bash. You missed it, bro."

Carson shook himself awake and looked over at his

intoxicated roommate.

Andy galloped pass a Wayne Gretzky's poster thumb-tacked on the back of the door. Andy spoke. "A lady belonging on an outlaw's motorcycle, tats and piercings across her body, wrapped her arms around me and said, "'You ready for the late night special?' Don't believe me, ask Jivin."

Jivin iced alongside Andy on the hockey team. They were buddies. Carson yawned.

"Andy?" Carson's eyes were almost fully open again. He couldn't believe his so called friend, or roommate for that matter, had planned to do it above him while he slept.

"I would have brought her. Luckily Jivin intervened and brought me to my senses. 'My bad' I said to her. I was sober enough to understand that our little fling was off. 'Sorry, wild thang. Dates off', I said."

"Andy?" Carson's eyes were almost fully open again. He could not believe his so called roommate had planned to "do it" above him while he slept.

Andy continued. "'What?' she said. She took her arms off me and moved away. 'I can't believe this. I'm never messing with any of you college junkies ever again', she said.'"

Carson listened as Andy explained her wardrobe—a leather vest showing tatted up arms and short shorts, revealing a nice body. On her hip, the word *Rose* was tattooed down her thigh, covered by her shorts.

"With wide hips, this tattoo led to her name. Even Jivin couldn't blame me for wanting to know the rest of it."

"Dude how old was she?" asked Carson.

Andy closed the door. "Young Enough."

Carson went back to his studying in a useless effort to prepare for his exam. He put his books back where they belonged and cut the light to his lamp off. He intentionally forgot to tell Andy about his mail. It was too late and he was too tired. Besides he'd noticed it when he went to sleep.

That's if he ever got to it. Carson pulled the covers over himself and tightened his pillows to his ears, trying to ignore the pukes of Andy's hangover from the bathroom.

—

"I don't know," Carson said for the eighth time. "Why would I want to tamper with your shit? What could you possibly have that would benefit me?"

"Someone had to open it," Andy pushed, shaking the envelope in the air. "Mail doesn't just open itself!"

One of the envelopes had been opened so Andy was curious to know what it had contained. It was from Pittsburgh, Andy knew that for sure, but he didn't have any affiliation with Pennsylvania whatsoever. "Last night I didn't notice them because I was too wasted to take caution to anything," he said.

"I don't have time for this, I got a test to get to and I am running late," Carson said. He wanted to be in class by seven and it was already the hour.

He grabbed his book bag and left in flip flops. On his way out, he called back to Andy: "Check with some of the others—Tim, Jivin, Sid, or Danny. It had to be one of them because the mail was already here when I came in like I told you."

He scooped up a banana and a bottle of Zephyrhills

on his way out to the bus stop just as the campus Bull Runner was coming. The Bull was the USF mascot.

On the bus he took out his cell phone and dialed Nadia's number. Nadia could wish him good luck before the test. But he got voice mail after three rings. He put his cell phone back into his pocket and reviewed his math material for the rest of the way.

The University of South Florida. The Bulls. As a teenager entering his freshmen year, Carson's goal was to land a good job by his junior year. Well, about that plan...

When he got into Professor Skoler's classroom, the exams were already on every desk space, the packets faced down so no one could see them.

Class started almost as soon as Carson took a seat. Carson was usually the late one to class every day, but not today; there was too much on his plate.

The professor started by addressing the exam and his expectations. Professor Skoler warned of testing rules and directions, and then said, "At this time you can flip your test packets over and start."

"What if you went to Super Bash last night and you're still half dozed?" a girl sitting in the front row asked. "Can you sit this one out?"

Carson recognized this girl as Sandy, the girlfriend of Danny, who was seated right beside her. This Bash had to be the same party that Andy had attended.

"You can start your test or you can leave," said Professor Skoler, walking to her desk.

Carson flipped his test over and began to hear the scribbles and scratches that went along with Calculus from around the room. The first question was easy and Carson got through the first page in a whiff. The next set of problems was harder and the six page test only got difficult as he advanced.

Nonetheless, he grinded out the hard problems and finished the exam with four people still testing. He handed his test to Professor Skoler who said, "Your Welcome" and stacked it along with the rest of the exams. Class ended and Sandy and Danny turned in blank tests with just their names on it.

Eying the nearby Subway, Carson had a good 15 minutes until his next class. Professor

Skoler promised to have everyone's grades posted on their University accounts by 7:00 tomorrow, but the contradicting Professor couldn't guarantee anything. Carson looked backed to stare at some notable sorority girls when he bumped into someone in a purple shirt.

"Hey watch where you're going!"

"Sid?" Carson recognized, having gained his balance. He had bumped into Sid! Sid was wearing a button down with white skinny jeans. Sid's wardrobe always stood out. His wardrobe was always Note-A-Bull.

"Carl? Oh, excuse me pawl. I didn't mean to truck you." Sid liked to joke. Joke as if he could really run someone over with his weaseled frame.

Carson saw the Calculus book in his hands. "That's right. You have Professor Skoler's exam next period too, don't you? I forgot."

"Yeah. Didn't you just come from taking it? Hard, was it?"

"It was. But if you studied you should be able to grind your way through."

"So you think you think did swell?" Sid said.

"I won't know until tomorrow, dude."

"Say, last night," the Connecticut native cackled in a suspect tone. "Did Andy get his mail?"

"You mean the envelopes that were torn and ripped empty? What do you know about that mail? Talk Sid."

Sid placed both of his arms around his books and put his arms to his chest. He had a strong fire in his eyes as he glared at Carl, as if trusting him to guard his closet.

"Okay but if I tell, promise not to tell anyone," Sid said. "When I checked the mail yesterday they were all for Andy. He hasn't checked his box in ages so the mail man emptied his collection in the Beta shipment room. And then I saw the one from the Pittsburgh Penguins. I was flabbergasted. I had to open it and when I saw they were inviting him to an open tryout next month after he graduates, I couldn't let him get it."

It was no doubt that Andy gave Sid a hard time in the dorm. But to go this far—it was a little drastic and spiteful. This was a guy's future at stake. Carson's roommate future at that.

"Sid, what's your problem? You can't tamper with people's future like that. And to go in another man's mail..."

"This will serve as retribution for all those times he teased me. Let's see who'll be laughing when he's flipping burgers with a college degree, if he even gets that."

"C'mon Sid. We're talking about hockey here. What else can Andy do without the ice.

You know I'll have to tell him about this."

Despite his excessive partying and poor academics, Andy was quite the hockey player. As the third ranked goalie in college hockey, Andy had made a name for himself by stopping puts and being responsible for shutouts.

When he was on the ice, he was whole, at peace, and couldn't see himself doing anything else.

Sid swooshed his Calculus book to his side and started for the university Research/Library center. "I thought you'd be with me on the holdout. You've seen how he has treated me. If you tell, I swear you're in the same boat!" Sid said threateningly. "Don't tell or Else!"

"Sid this has nothing to do with me—" Carson tried running after him but the hall was too crowded. "Sid!"

Sid was gone. There was no use chasing or yelling after him. *Curses*, thought Carson.

The next morning Carson awoke at six in the morning eager to see his test grade. They wouldn't be posted until seven a.m. so he went ahead and took a rare morning shower. Andy didn't come home last night and when Carson got out the shower he heard the door open and saw his broke, busted, and disgusted roommate come in and shut the door with a drink in his hand.

"Andy?" Carson shot. "I have something you need to know about that open mail."

"What? You flushed it down the toilet?"

How about I turn you in for curfew? Carson thought.

"No man, listen. Sid checked the mail yesterday and tore open your envelopes to find out that the Pittsburgh Penguins, I believe you know who they are, invited you to open tryouts. He confessed everything to me yesterday at school."

Andy took a sip from his drink, a mixture that only God could know. "Kidding, right? He told you that?" Andy took another drink. Drinking was his protection against problems. It was his protection against the future.

"No kidding dude. I swear on a stack of bibles. The

Pittsburgh Penguins want you, Andy Demingdes, to try out for their team after you graduate."

Andy took the drink away from his mouth and shook his head. "Why would that faggot tear my mail up and hide it? I should tear his face up to pieces!"

Andy ripped the door open! "Just let me get a hold of that faggot!" The door opened with a force so strong that his drink fell to the floor.

"Andy Wait!" Carson pleaded. He ran to the door, albeit the puddle of beer near the doorway. "Stop! You don't want to do something you will regret. The best thing to do is pretend like you don't know anything about it. You should get all the information you need from the Penguins office and organization. Then make a spot on their roster. Throw the shit right back on him!"

Andy's right arm was in the clutch of Carson's. "You think so?" he asked, losing the anger.

"Absolutely," said the shirtless scholar. "When you make the team you'll have the coward doing back flips in his grave!"

"You know what, I think you're right. I'm going to do just that. From what's left of the envelope I have a pretty good idea of the Penguins contact office. I'll drive there right now. No more beers and partying for me and I will start training after I come back."

Andy passed his roommate, stepped over the puddle of beer, and grabbed some clothes and all three pieces of mail that was left.

Carson watched him walk back out. "What about your class today?" he asked.

"I should make it back in time."

Carson said, "Andy do not tell Sid I told you anything."

"Of course not." the athlete said, and then went down stairs. Carson heard Andy's Ford Shelby rumble up and away.

Seven o'clock came fast and Carson logged in to his USF email to check his Calculus grade.

"What?" Carson blurted out. The margin under the Calc Skill Exam was blank. No score was there. Once again, Professor Skoler never guaranteed anything.

Carson gathered himself then caught the bus back to campus. He didn't have Calculus today, but he was desperate to see his grade. He needed this exam score. Those student loans he took out would all be for granted if he failed.

The classroom was empty as he walked in. Professor Skoler saw him first.

"Mr. Effields, is that you?" she said, adjusting her eyeglasses.

"The very one. Do you have the exam grades in yet?"

Carson couldn't help taking in a fresh look at her breasts. She tried to hide them from her students but she was simply "top heavy."

"Oh yes. I wasn't able to put them online because of some of technical difficulties. I remember your score. You scored the highest in the class."

"Really! What did I get?"

"A 58," Skoler recalled.

"That's horrible!"

"Apparently horrible is better than everyone else." She brushed her black hair with her hand. "Next class we will be moving on to the next lesson. You kids will just have to do better on the next assessment."

"Yes Mam'," Carson said. And he left the class.

"*Fat Witch*!" he screamed inside himself. How could she lead his hopes and then take them all away? She didn't post the test grades on purpose.

Carson felt horrible. It was a good chance he'd flunk this semester now.

Then he saw Sid. Sid was land surfing on his skateboard.

Avoiding Sid, Carson snatched his cell phone out his pocket and pressed redial from when he called Nadia earlier. After the fourth ring Nadia picked up, and then hung up just as fast. What a Bitch!

"Nadia! Nadia! Pick up!" Carson begged. He didn't get it. Why was she dodging him?

"Looking for old girl Nadia?" came the feminine voice of Sid. "I just saw her with this hunk guy in the library. Nadia was all curled up on him."

"Where?"

"Over at the Marshall Center up by the Ballroom. They were a sight to see. Nadia is a player, she has guys on schedules. You're just another statistic to her. Probably why you can never get any."

How the hell did this half queer know if he had gotten laid by Nadia yet?

Sid read Carson's mind. "Oh please. It's obvious. Listen bro, I would just quit her if I were you."

The hot steam from Sid's Starbucks coffee cup hit Carson in the face as Sid skated by on his long board. "Ha," Sid laughed as Carson, again, watched him leave.

—

Days ago Carson and Sid had been best college buddies. But Sid's female qualities had conquered him, destroying roots that would never be the same. Ms. Skoler and Nadia had complicated his life further and it seemed effortless on their behalf. The women in his life were unpredictable and it was times like these where he swore women made Calculus.

OVERWEIGHT

—

The basketball gymnasium of Saints High School, Home of the Spartans, had been sparked last night with waves of wild fans, making the stands on each side of the gym wild and crazy. In fact, it had been so steaming with buzz and so raucous with attendants choosing between sides of the gym and the best seats that the janitors decided not to go through with their usual pre-cleaning practices and put them off until after the game ended and the wild fans had fled the gym.

The Mighty Spartans as staff members referred to them were known for its elite boys' Varsity program. And it was this unfortunate fact that Feta MacBook and the rest of her custodial team resented. The talented basketball squad had the fan base of a NBA team and attracted swarms wherever they played. Wherever the team left, a horrible scene trailed behind. Whether playing a home or away game, the mighty Spartans never ceased to attract an epic number of fans that ramped and raved and trashed the gymnasiums they were in.

Through it all—rain, snow, or shine—the janitors had to renew the scene that lay before them.

As always, the job would seem impossible at first, but they'd gradually defeat the monster. Return to their homes with their heads held high, dignities intact. Anything for the family. But only at $7.25—minimum wage.

Ms. MacBook cursed the basketball team as she entered the gymnasium and started cleaning an unfinished section. Although the janitors were aided by the help of staff members and student volunteers from the National Honor Society, they were unable to get the gym in order for the next day of school and were forced to section off a portion of the gym.

It was evident to Ms. MacBook and the custodian staff that the town of Saint Libby had no place better to be last night.

"Why don't they try going to work for starters?" Ms. MacBook and the Janitors scowled at one another.

Usually the custodial team would get an early start on the gymnasium and finish the job the same night. Yesterday's match had been a big game that was highly anticipated for some time now. The Warthogs were the Spartans opponents, and both were undefeated. A big crowd had been expected and the prediction could not have been more accurate. The game proved to be a monumental sell-out, the population of the gym easily over capacity. God bless the janitors. Lord knows they had their work cut out for them.

Ms. MacBook finished cleaning the gym. Each janitor had been assigned a section to clean by the Principal. Hopefully, her co-workers were still cleaning parts of the school too so she wouldn't look like the weakest link.

Feta MacBook was a solid, high blood pressure ridden woman. She had specifically requested to finish the gym. She preferred cleaning open spaces because they were easier to maneuver through and quicker to clean than the claustrophobic hallways and classrooms.

As Ms. MacBook approached the back door to the

gymnasium building, she heard what sounded like the asi-nine voices of teenaged girls.

Opening the door to the left wing of the gym, she shoved her weight on the door and swung it open. She gingerly limped into the lengthy hallway that was lit by the sun from outside, and then stood there looking at two girls as they smirked at her.

Ms. MacBook placed her cleaning supplies on the ground. The smaller of the two girls erupted in laughter.

"Damn she's A *Fat Fuck*!" the girl bust out, laughing so hard she was almost unable to speak.

The other girl, who was much bigger and broader than the first, chuckled and said, "You better shut up before that woman goes Sumo wrestling us for lunch."

And at that they both thundered in laughter.

Ms. MacBook bent down to reach her broom. She would sweep up this distance first, then get the hallway that connected the locker room and the gymnasium. She stared the girls down and watched them chuckle at her. Swiftly, Ms. MacBook asked at the girls, "What were you doing in the boys' locker room?"

The girls laughed even harder now.

The unfazed janitor shook her head then proceeded to clean the rest of the hallway. The young girls taunting hadn't affected her. Many times immature kids and child-ish adults openly teased her about her weight. Yes, she was obese and nothing was going to change that.

But what she really wanted to know was why the doors to the boys' locker room were still flapping. She looked up at the ridiculous girls nearing the end of the hallway, geared down in sportswear. The girls had been in the boys' locker room, the next and last area she was assigned to clean.

—

The girls were still laughing when they approached the doors ending the hallway. If a three word term could describe a friendship then Maliya was ace, Angely was boon, and trouble was coon.

"Did you see the thighs on that animal?" Maliya, the smaller of the girls, was still laughing, still unable to get over that overweight janitor lady.

"It's a wonder she's able to work here and clean things," Angely said. "That's if she even cleans it by herself. She probably gets helped by other janitors."

Angely was a step or two behind Maliya and they were now at the doors to the end of the hallway. "I don't think I've ever seen her."

"Me neither," Maliya contorted as she shoved her sport bag against the door, popping it open wide enough for them both. "I've never really noticed any of the janitors. Just her fat ass."

And she laughed again.

"I bet she'll be the last sole to leave school today. Even after Mr. Taylor."

Mr. Taylor was the school principal and he gained popularity from showcasing and representing his High School's basketball program. Games were bragging rights so wherever the Spartans went, he followed.

"I bet that cry baby is still crying his pants out over last night's game," Maliya said.

Before the games kickoff, Principal Taylor would get up and boast that his Varsity squad was the best in the nation and were superior to competition. At away games Principal Taylor would trail in behind the team and Coach Jennings was left to suffer through Principal Taylor's prep rallies. It was his second year as principal and he had become the cheerleader that his Varsity basketball team didn't need.

The girls reached the school weight room. Otherwise known as the athletic training center, the weight room was enclosed inside the campus. School was over for today, so without the congested hallways, the girls reached the facility in no time.

Maliya opened the door to the weight room. Painted freshly green and yellow, the weight room had recently been completed to commemorate the arrival of the Spring sport season. Both girls filed in and the door closed shut behind them with a "Bang."

Maliya and Angely flopped their gym bags in the weight room and settled themselves onto spaces on the floor and stretched. Maliya had on a light practice suit that she wore to practice. She was a junior at Saints High. Angely was a senior. Angely adjusted the headphones in her ears that ran to an I-pod device.

On the way to the weight room, Maliya spotted a tall man coming from the inner side of campus and enter the hallway to the locker room. Maliya noticed the man was dressed professionally and was walking with a purpose. She tried to alert her friend but she was busy with her cellular device and couldn't hear her. Frustration was written across his face and from the glimpse she got, he looked like the boys' varsity coach from last night.

Pulling her shoulders together with her arms over her head, Maliya started talking about the game.

"You know I hate what happened last night. Everybody at the school does. And since Mr. Taylor was so close to the team, it's no big surprise he's taken the loss like he has. It will be a while before he gets over it."

Angely took one head phone out of her left ear. "Yeah, I hear you. They were due to lose."

"I can't blame him. I mean I'd be mad too if I cared if the boys happened to lose. That last play was horrible. A foul should have been called. How could the referee not call a foul on that drive Jeffrey took?"

Last night's game ended on a controversial "no call." With the Golden Knights up one point with seconds to go, Jeffrey Dimes, the star of Saints High, made a strong break for the basket as a smaller defender hacked him in the air, killing his control of the ball.

The closest referee, who appeared to be sleep walking throughout the whole ordeal, put his whistle in his mouth, took it back out, and watched as the game clock ticked zero. The building rocked in disbelief and a piece of Principal Taylor's sole went with him after watching his bread and butter be handed their first loss of the season. A number of fans flung food at the fleeing referee, and after the game all he could say was, "The player in motion still had a decent shot at making the basket after the defender applied contact."

Angely said, "Me and the girls still can't believe you went to that game. We made a pact and you broke it."

Albeit their friendship, the girls were also teammates on the Lady Saints basketball team and since their games were basically a ghost town, they had vowed to never attend any of the boy's games, in revolt. Since no one was attending their games, why should they support the boys?

Who cared *how* good they were?

"I already told some of the girls in school today that I went," claimed Maliya, stretched out. "I couldn't help it. How could anyone miss a game like that one?"

Maliya watched her friend remove earphones from her ears then put them in her bag. Then she took out a I-pod and blasted Nicki Minaj. *Pink Friday* serenaded from inside the weight room.

"You should have never made the pack. Everyone would like to see Jeffrey play," Angely educated. "It's the principle."

Maliya hovered over to the windows of the weight room. She could see a gang of emo-looking kids who could pass for Gothics. Though she couldn't hear them, she could read lips and she interpreted one of the girls saying: "You boys are dummies. You only care about your own boyish needs."

She watched one of the boys grab a girl and grasp her buttocks and put his tongue in her ear. She watched them pass the chain of buildings and classrooms.

Coincidentally, Principal Taylor's office was not far from the weight room. Mr. Taylor's office was four rooms ahead of the weight room where he had come straggling in after witnessing the epic defeat of his Varsity basketball team yesterday night. He had been so late to work that someone else did the morning announcements.

Principal Taylor was a divorced man trying to patch his heart up; so basketball had become his everything. Rumor was that he'd been so dazed when the team suffered their first loss that he'd committed a bowel movement on himself after several shots of liquor.

And the spirit of the Jeffrey Dimes had been immensely damaged. When the game ended after the controversial no-call, he kept his head down, not talking or looking anyone in the eye. He was so hurt by the loss that he did not come to school the next day.

"Anyways, we got a game tomorrow." Angely turned her music down and walked to where Maliya was surveying a bench press set. "You ready to bench press?" Angely asked.

After looking out the window onto the empty Saint's High campus, Maliya had gone to where the bench press sets were. "I still have to check the condition of our workout material. You can't depend on these weights. They're dangerous."

From the fourth game of the lady's season up until now, the girls came into the weight room every day before their games. They would work out and stretch, and lastly they'd test their strength on the bench press machine. The stronger the better.

"Time to hit the bench. Ready Freddy?"

Maliya couldn't hear Angela over the volume of Nicki Minaj. But, again, she could read lips. She nodded, "Yes."

"Everything looks good," Maliya said, checking the equipment. "Let's do this." Maliya had finalized her inspection of the equipment and was ready to lift.

She slid her slim body under the bench press set and began to lift the forty five pound bar. "We'll start light then grind to the heavier stuff. We'll max out at the end."

Angely didn't hear her over the music but she didn't need to. She knew the drill. It was the same routine they'd been doing at the start of the year.

So for the next half hour, they lifted, pushed and racked. As Maliya promised, they got to an easy start and worked their way up the weight. Angely racked for Maliya and Maliya racked for Angely. They took turns and at one point they were at 145 pounds on the bar.

Then they agreed that Angely should max out next.

"I'm going for a high of 150," Angely said. "It's all or nothing."

Maliya racked the appropriate weight onto the bar. One hundred and fifty pounds.

The portable music device had been placed on an adjacent weight set next to where the girls were lifting and Angely had turned the volume down by a few notches.

"Get a clean grip on the bar and bring it straight up. If you feel you can't lift one full rep, don't try it. I'm not sure I'll be able to pull this off you if it comes down to it."

Angely pressed the bar up, getting the weight in her grasp as Maliya got into spotting position.

Angely held the weight in her clutch for a little less than a second. It definitely was heavy. If she could get it to bounce off of her chess she thought she may be able to overpower it.

She could feel the power, the mighty strength it would take to lift one full rep. *I think I can…I think I can…*she thought, bringing the bar down.

*I think I can…*Angely thought she could. But she thought wrong.

Halfway to her chess, the weight of the bar became too much. It became overweight. Her strength collapsed. All 155 pounds of steel dropped to her chess. Maliya couldn't even react.

It was too much weight to lift: Overweight!

"No!" Maliya rushed to grab the bar from Angely's chest but the only thing she could do was raise it high enough above her chest, making breathing room.

Maliya panicked. "Oh God! I knew this was a bad idea!"

"Push with me! Push!"

Maliya then released her grip from the bar and raced for the door, knocking the I-pod onto the ground, stopping the music.

"HELP! HELP!" Maliya screamed!

——

Stoned from another long day of work, Ms. MacBook sluggishly walked out of the locker room to the school courtyard. With any luck, there would be a few other janitors in the clock out lounge who would be late in their cleanings so she would not look like a slow poke again. From the gym to the lounge was the shortest stretches on campus, a good thing considering her hindered mobility.

When she entered the boy's locker room, the same locker room the teen girls came out of, a questionable smell lingered in the air. Moving inside, Ms. MacBook noted that it was the smell of marijuana and had been caused by more than one person.

And then she saw the tall boy sitting on a bench without a shirt on.

Ms. MacBook recognized him from the basketball games. Jeffrey Dimes, they called him. She couldn't help remembering him because the men janitors would praise his basketball prowess.

Ms. MacBook asked him, "What are you doing here boy?"

"Nothing." came the hard reply, flicking something

from his fingers.

"What is that awful smell? And why in the world don't you have a shirt on?"

"No reason. I left the house like this. Look it's none of your business." He folded his arms around his chest and looked at the floor.

"You've got so much going for you kid, don't ruin it like this."

Ms. MacBook started to clean the locker room.

Jeffrey remained there with his head down. As Ms. MacBook finished and walked out the door she said, "Get yourself outta here kid," then threw a shirt up at him.

The door to the Boys' locker room had just closed when a tall athletic looking man with a whistle around his neck approached Ms. MacBook.

"Did you see a kid in there?" he asked. "Goes by the name Jeffrey Dimes? Seen him when you were cleaning up? I'm the coach of his team. Coach Jennings."

Ms. MacBook shook her head and said, "No."

"Very well," said Coach Jennings. "Thank you for your time." Coach left the other way out of the school.

Ms. MacBook heard the boy leave a little bit after, and she turned to see him in the shirt she'd given him as he headed out the gym. She had saved the boy from his coach, saved the boy from screwing up his basketball career, a fate he would appreciate down the line.

Before she could grasp the full magnitude of what happened, Ms. MacBook heard someone shouting cries from a room to her left.

"Help! Help! Help!" the frantic pleads only got louder. When she turned, Ms. MacBook saw that the screams were coming from the weight room. She zoomed to the door, going as fast as her body would allow and almost ended up colliding with a small girl.

"HELP! I NEED HELP!" The girl was screaming and pointing. But it wasn't any girl; it was one of the teens who had laughed at her earlier in the hallway!

"Here! My friend in here needs Help! She can't push the weight from off her! Please!"

Then Ms. MacBook looked up to see the other girl—the more healthier one—lying on her back with her breath held, crowded with an impossible weight on her chess, struggling, dying.

The sight itself was enough for the janitor to dash for the defenseless athlete, grab the bench press bar the girl was holding and rack it, hoping the girl was alright.

And there Ms. MacBook and Maliya stood staring at the gasping Angely.

"Angely, are you OK?" Maliya asked.

She was gasping, choking on air, unable to answer, to talk.

"Cool it!" Ms MacBook exclaimed. "Let her catch her breath before anything."

So they both watched and studied the mercurial Angely. For a moment, she appeared lifeless. Then she started coughing up something vicious, clearing her throat. Gaining consciousness, snapping back to life.

Angely looked up to where Maliya was still frozen and said: "I thought I was going to die. Right then and there."

Ms. MacBook was concerned. "You had an unsustainable amount of weight on you for a short amount of time. And while your neck and throat may feel fine, you may have suffered heart and chess damage."

"No," Angely said, "hearts fine. Really. Everything

feels fine. I should be thanking you."

Angely was now sitting straight up in the bench. She watched as the big janitor lady gleamed at her friend, almost like a mother nursing her sick child.

"Very well then," Ms. MacBook said. She stepped a few steps away from the bench press set. "I'd like for you girls to know I am aware of your little extracurricular activity you were involved in today in the boy's locker room. I saw Jeffrey Dimes in there. And the smell—you had been smoking weed."

"How do you know who Jeffrey Dimes is?" Maliya asked.

"Everyone in this school knows who Jeffrey is," Ms. MacBook said. "I think he is one of the top players in the nation. And, because of your careless ways, he was almost caught by his coach and his basketball career could have been over, all because of some weed. But I intervened before Coach came into the locker room and I told him no one was inside. Coach left and later so did that Dimes kid—in a T-shirt I'd given him."

Both girls had blank expressions on their faces from what they had been told.

Then, Maliya spoke. "His shirt was off but we didn't do anything. Trust me. He had come to the school with no shirt on and when he saw us he wanted to smoke."

"I damn sure hope not because it's not worth it. Drugs and sex is not worth it at your age. Enjoy these years and try not to grow up too fast. That's what happened to me and I ended up dropping out of high school."

A shivering noise muffled from outside and they listened to the low moans of Principal Taylor: "Lightning never strikes twice!" he was saying. "A team always learns from defeat. We will lose from no team from here on out!"

"Poor Principal Taylor. He's in delusion. Gone Borderline skit-so," Angely said.

Looking down, Maliya noticed the right leg of the janitor lady who had saved her best friends life. A metallic bracing coveted where her left leg was supposed to be. The hero was an amputee.

"Miss, what's your name?"

"Names Fetta MacBook. But I suppose you call me Ms. MacBook. For you own sake."

"Ms. MacBook what happened to your leg?"

"Same thing that happened to my whole body. A few years back I was diagnosed with a terrible disease that spread throughout my body. Caused me to gain weight by the day. I gained close to a hundred and fifty pounds. It got so bad in my left leg I had to have surgery but they ended up cutting it off. Giving me a fake leg in its place. I used to be as skinny as you all in school."

"Really?"

"Really. Played sports and all."

"Ms. MacBook?" called Angely.

"Yes, child."

"I want to apologize–"

"We want to apologize," Maliya corrected.

"We want to apologize," Angely continued, "for laughing at you and thank you for saving my life. Otherwise, the situation could've been a lot uglier."

"For real. Old coo-coo Taylor definitely would not have been in his right mind to help us," Maliya replied.

"Girls instead of thanking me you should request an adult to be in the weight room at all times after school."

"Wait Ms. MacBook. Excuse me, but why don't you just be a coach?" Maliya asked.

"I can't," Ms. MacBook said.

"Why?"

"I don't get paid enough," she said, then opened the door to the weight room and disappeared.

PARALLEL PEOPLE

—

"**S**he—yes—her, finished the trial ahead of the rest of them," I say, directing the rank sergeant toward the fit girl with the fair skin under the pavilion. I lead the Activities Commander to her, standing amongst the rest of the Air Force bound girls.

"Sergeant," she salutes her right hand in notable execution.

"Commander here would like to chat with you about your conditioning," I say.

With arms folded behind his back, Commander takes control: "Young lady, I don't have to tell you you're in splendid shape," he says. "And to me your physicality is of particular interest. Every year I pick someone new for this privilege. You girls are required to pass the upcoming strength test. So as an added benefit, I'd like to name you captain of your squad in the event that the rest of your team move on to join the Air Force as well."

Gazing around at her fellow soldiers, she sobers as females make envious faces. When hate circulated the bloodstream, there was no telling. Pun intended.

But I knew she could read them: "Lucky her."

This is why she would make a better leader. Because she could read people. "Sir, I accept sir," she says.

"Good. I will talk to you more shortly," the Commander finishes, looking up at me for the queue.

"All right everyone," I began. "Today's obstacle training is done. You can leave but don't forget to do your work outs and whatnot. The last week here of basic training is almost upon us."

I salute, breaking them from basic training. Manana'. Till tomorrow.

"Sir Yes, sir!" The girls broke from the session.

I watch Commander take the girl off to converse one on one.

She was the only girl I ever seen complete the demo like she has. And I'd been in this stint at the National Air Force Reserve basic training station as a top line drill sergeant for a while now. I nicknamed her Sonic. She breezed through the maze and when she got to the wall she climbed it clean like a lizard, and then sprinted to the end of the trial. We didn't time her but damn could she move!

There final assessment maze was upcoming. This was mandatory to pass or else they didn't get inducted into the Air Force. We might as well congratulate her now.

Commander wraps it up with Sonic and she floats toward me after their conversation.

I ask her, "What was Commander talking about, Sonic?"

"It's confidential. Respect my grind."

"Child, please," I say to her as I go toward the vending machines which is near the tent hut that I live in.

"I may take your instructor job in the future."

I spin around, committing a 180 degree turn. "He said that?"

"Quote on quote. In so many words he did," Sonic says.

Resurrecting something about Commander, I stop in my tracks. Commander is slick. He is a hypocrite and can sometimes be ridiculous. Commander can easily blend in any surrounding, making himself appear unnoticed—like the true chameleon he is.

Turning around I say to Sonic, "Commander is a two faced fool. Remember that. Try not to take him too strong."

"I was just saying," said Sonic, following me to the machines.

"And I'm just saying be careful. The dude's a fox."

I buy a drink with a Kennedy fifty cents coin and can hear Sonic's light footsteps behind me. Carrying my drink in hand, I have a strong urge to test her. Let's quiz this Miss Sonic the hedgehog.

"What are your plans after you become a reserved soldier? Assuming you pass the final trial. You know a bone could break during your exhibition trial or something awful like that. I've seen it happen before."

"There you go jinxing me," she says. "You can pay for my retirement. Along with a disability check from the military service, I'll be good to go."

I smile as I walk across the pieces of wooden streaks: So she has done her homework. My previous station had me with Marines in Paris Island. The Marines were no brainiac's from what I could tell. If they have one it was peanut size. None of the Marines had any idea of how the military operated and the benefits it had to tap into.

Nor was Sonic a scarecrow either.

Sonic's rear end belonged to an ebony vixen off the last Ebony magazine cover. True Story. Sonic's butt was plump enough to be two story's high. Slim hips maid her upper and lower body separate perfectly like a mermaid washed upon shore.

Curly hair gave her red carpet skin a look like she'd live forever.

"Keep a plan B," I say. "I won't tell you anything wrong."

"Yes sir," said Sonic mockingly. She follows me inside my small tent hut.

"No joke," I said. "My grandmother taught me to read at a very young age. In case she passed, I would always know how to cook on my own. 'A man that can read can always prepare a meal for himself. Follow the Directions, Caveman!' I will always remember her for that."

Sonic looks the tent over then says, "I hear you Sergeant. But there's a chance I never go to war. Reserved military soldiers sometimes never see action. My training could all be in vain. Can't blame me for not putting my eggs in one basket."

"When I was stationed in Paris Island the level of stupidity I encountered was discerning. At an alarming rate, the Marine basic trainees were clueless to what they'd do if tragedy struck."

As I rummage through my landscaping tools to trim up the shrubs upon my tent, Sonic does a mean stretch. Her booty arches out as if saying, "Take me. I'm yours."

Sonic says: "Do you know where I come from. It would be crazy not to be aware of all my options after I join the Air Force Reserve."

"That's good Sonic. You have a good head on your shoulders. And so does Sonic the cartoon head!"

"Whatever. I learned from the mistakes my brother made. He dropped out of school and the world ate him up and spat him back out in one meal. He thought about going to the Marines before he got in too deep. I knew I could not be him."

I try my best to stay calm and steady as she undulates in stretch moves that are beyond my description. Picture yoga classes, minus the aerobics clothes. It is difficult peeping out the corner of my eye as I am doing. Shit, she knew what she was doing!

"At least you had the option to learn from someone," I say, heading out. "My grandma raised me and taught me everything she knew. She was all I ever knew."

Sonic bends, doing a semi-split behind my back. Cheater! I wasn't even looking.

What are the chances that Sonic could be coming on to me? I mean am a towering six foot four inches tall and I weigh a roaring two hundred pounds of rock solid muscle. I am used to having my way with women. I remain single as a relationship is pointless with all the promiscuous females I meet overseas.

As I close around my tent, I ask: "When basic training ends next week, you will be doing what?"

"I will be attending the local technical school," she says. "There I will study for my technical certification to become an analyst to help out my family at home. Originally I wanted to go to technical school in the first place. But when an Air Force Recruiter came to my English Honors class, a light bulb suddenly flicked on in my head. Even though my family promised to help me pay for college, I had to make the right decision for myself. The Air Force was too much to pass up. I will go to technical school and wait for the Reserve to ring me in for deployment."

"Sounds like a plan," I said. "You have anyone special back home?"

"Me? No."

"Why not?"

I had to ask.

"All I saw were girls getting ruined by boys. I want to get my education first and a better job before a man comes into my life."

I knew she was smart, but not this smart. "Damn ambitious girl! I understand where you're coming from. Growing up, my grandmother always told me whatever a man gives a woman she can make it greater. 'Give her groceries, and she will make you a meal. Give her a house and she will give you a home. Give her your heart, she will return you with love. But if you give her crap, be prepared to receive a ton of garbage!'"

Sonic laughs out loud. "LOL! You had a crazy gramps, Jess!"

"She was the best," I say, reflecting on Joyce Cole, my grandmother, who forever lives inside of me. "It's true though. A man and a woman are an unstoppable force. Why do you think being the first lady of the United States is such an important role?"

Blowing steam, I chip away at an overgrown cactus. Thorns scatter as twitches fall onto the earth.

"I'm leaving Sgt. Jess," said Sonic, "I won't be happy if one of those thorns stitches me up."

She marches off in her purple designer Nike's. "Salute soldier."

I am not fantasizing. A real cat woman walk works before me. Sonic shows off her fine body as she leaves, detail so deep in that torso of hers that I consider it the most underrated part of a chick's body. Sonic walks away but I can't help but admire her nature.

Signs of chemistry were between us. Jess and Sonic? Please. And us talking how we did—it happened so quickly. We never talked so long.

Damn today sucks!

So I am just about done with my gardening. The evening ejects out oven baked heat. Sweat trickles down my shoulders as I hack, perspiring with purpose. To add injury to insult, my service boots drench in the irrigation residue left from morning skiing.

"Sergeant Jess!"

My name is yelled from the side of the tent. Above, a large shadow partakes my view and the large figure of Boss-man Kernel, my overseer, is revealed.

While gradually keeping my progress, I yell out: "Hi Boss. Need me?"

"Why didn't you tell me Commander came Here!" Kernel was madder than a hot head coach. "He slipped in on me trying to put on shampoo!"

"Men get dandruff?" I ask.

"We do but women never know." He is cross. "Just like women never fart around us. Jess, I am serious here! I am legitimately displeased with your work!"

Kernel beefs, moving to face me.

Kernel intimidated everyone. Huge forearms and an AK-47 loaded chest made him look like he had on a bullet proof at all the time. He confronts me man to man, a cross face challenging me just a couple feet away.

"I apologize boss, but the girl who Commander selected needed me. Supply and demand. She wanted to talk." I diagnosed.

Might as well tell the truth, lying would only dig a deeper grave for me.

Of all people, I was not scared of Kernel. I couldn't be. My background and all I saw as a kid testified to that. I come from a place where I grew up with my head down, ashamed of all the fake people I saw. My grandmother raised me to keep my head up but the more I did, the more pain I saw, stressing me down, sucking my sole away. I walk a thin line. And still level headed. I saw people try to break my stride.

"For your slip up, Run Four Miles! None Stop!"

"What?" I reply stupidly.

Back in my hometown, whack peers thought they knew me. In actuality they didn't know the "flushings of their own toilet."

Zero. Nothing. Not even a number.

"You heard me boy! What you deaf?"

"Yes. I heard." I cosign.

Eighteen years old entering the service, this military taught me how to keep my head strong, knocking insecurity's tough from my conscious. Military training made me stronger. The Air Force had made me into a man.

"Now!" Kernel says. "Run as ordered or else I'll put you on probation!"

By now I let the tool go, claiming the duty at hand void. Temptation opted inside my throat. At first, I begged to differ with Kernel. I wanted to argue. But risking probation was risky. It could cost me my instructor's job! I couldn't afford this. And I mean really. I needed the money.

So I settle. "Sir, Yes sir," I said, obeying his relentless annoyance.

That's another thing. At the moment, my boss was leading in votes for the officially most annoying person award. When he got hot, I regretted being around him. He was more aggravating than anybody I had ever been around. To me, he was more aggravating than scary.

I close the tent up and move on up the hill crest. Kernel is watching me the whole nine with a disgusted vigil on his face.

"I'll Be Watching to make sure you Do It!" Kernel said. "So will that Landscaper Lady up there."

The landscaper is digging weeds in indigo gloves. "How will she be able to keep up with me?"

"She has her ways."

Oh well. Shoot yourself. Off I go, taking pleasure in my jaunt. A mile was about five laps around the egg shaped desert hill. Four miles summed up to 20 laps. Though the desert is hot, four miles is very easy to do, particularly with someone in my shape & training. Tacos to a military trainer.

"Sir, yes sir," I salute off into the desert. The landscaper lady missed some spots where I start my run. An ant bed is established on the ground. Oh well, at least the grass is cut.

As I pull around the corner, Kernel goes to yelling again. I jog back to listen to what his fuss is about this time.

"...I don't understand you young people—you have the world to gain, yet you settle for the tree house! If success was a vertical line, y'all are that latitude line running parallel beside it. Excellence is what you kids should aim for! My generation would die to have the advantages you have..."

He is still yelling when I start back jogging. Blah, Blah, Blah. Kernel is pissed. I feel like I know where he is coming from, but where I come from I cannot be ashamed. Especially not of myself. I've heard comments like these before.

The generation before him would say the same thing about his.

The thick healthy landscaper lady with the indigo gloves is "Queen of the Hill" as she picks plants up on top of the hill, mothering my steady progress. So this is how she will scope me. The old lady will watch me from the Hill top while she attends to the garden.

As I am jogging, I lash out at Kernel hoping he can hear me. I holler: "I'm grown. Excuse whoever hates it."

I'm me. I do what I like.

The military is overrated.

...SYKE!

MONEY PROBLEMS

WEST COAST CUSTOMS

—

All real nigga's stayed on this side of East Los Angeles. Occasionally you could find a few Asians, Mexicans, and white people who stayed in the area, but for the most, it was Black. The few whites who lived in the neighborhood were exceptions, having weathered out the notorious wars of the Blood vs. Crip, police trespassing of sheer rancor, and the heat of the big city combined. It was definitely not *them* doing the terrorizing, they'd try and explain to SWAT, yet their property was getting vandalized. Despite its mean past, it remains prone to crime. Though Raw Hills had seen its worst, still it's no place for sightseeing. At night, it is the most dangerous place to be.

—

Pacing each other step by step, Junior and E-Dog walked real quickly while surrounded by sky scraping palm trees. Raw Hills Trail. They were coming from a Bachelor party at a hotel building that was rented out the whole night for the occasion. Beyond midnight, E-Dog bragged how he had pulled chicken heads despite all the darkness.

Bayson, a friend of E-Dog, was just a mediocre music producer at Decadence Recordings but when the executives of the company heard he was engaged, they agreed to help with a large portion of the wedding events. They hired 20 of the baddest strippers in California and many would do more than that. Catered food, dope music, and decorations were planned in advance including R.S.V.P letters sent to some of the biggest names in the music industry.

Many locals came and ten rooms were packed by eight. Arriving around nine, Junior and E-Dog nonetheless had a blast at the party even though it was tough maneuvering through the thick crowds of people. Both boys had gone to a table where a stripper was being awarded with cash by her onlookers below. Thrilled by the scene, the juveniles swiped some bills up from the table and moved to the next room which was a duplicate of the first. There were people dancing everywhere and Junior watched as E-Dog slid off with an exotic thing with the curves to kill. She had to be a stripper. Junior's highlight of the night came when three girls sandwiched him close by the DJ, one in front, another in the back, and one giving him mouth to mouth. Consuming too many bottles of Hennessy, Junior's bladder began to pay off. Before he knew it, it was time to use the restroom. He found one but it was locked. He put his ear to the door and could hear: "Oohs" and "Aahs" and "Fucks". J figured he knew who it was.

"Anybody in here?" No response confirmed his assumption. He knew his homeboy. He relieved himself through a window instead.

Later they met up outside after the cops came party pooping that this event was "vandalizing public property." Junior asked E-Dog, "How'd you get her?"

"*Shid,* the usual. I was like, told her I loved

'everythang about her."

"Magnum or Trojan?"

"You know I had to slide in wit yo' Trojans," E-Dog hinted. "USC All Day."

"My dog. I can't blame you. But that party went *Ham*, man," said Junior, better known as J-Play, as they walked like the west coast lynch mob was approaching from behind. Going back to their neck of the woods. Party over.

"It was '*aight*. But *A*, who says 'went ham' out here in L.A. 'tho fool?"

"I was just saying," was all J-Play could say. He, like the rest of Raw Hills, knew better than to detest against the motherfucking "Dog" when talking about proper west coast originality.

E-Dog grew up in Raw Hills. He was born there, raised there, shit—bred there. The culture of the swag setting L.A. was deeply engrained in him. From the way he talked, to the way he walked—"Nothing but the Truth." Having never been outside The Hills, he wasn't afraid to let it be known. E-Dog was proud of that.

"Say 'went in' or something, nigga."

The pair passed a water fountain. Everyone living near the proximity knew the fountains were void of water supply, the county abandoning the Trail for some years now since the height of the gang activities in the 80's. The only people who used the trail now were folks crossing sides or bombs looking for a quick spot to crash.

And gang members seeking crime.

E-Dog fixed his Los Angeles Dodger's snap-back cap—complimented by his James Worthy throwback. A young nigga got his fresh on. Believe that.

"But for real though, this L.A. You think I ever say

'went ham' in my verses?" E-Dog was chuckling now. "Tell you ain't from here."

Born to a family ruined by crack rock, E-Dog earned his street name by developing his rap reputation early on. The heavily jeweled and even more tattooed E-Dog had been rapping since he was a kid. To the up most, he fitted the profile of a west coast rapper. The streets nicknamed him E-Dog because he would eat beats like a stray dog. E-Dog dropped out of school in the 9th grade after becoming friends with J-Play. He looked up to a legend in Tupac. He lived in his OG uncle's trap house and became used to guns. Therefore, he learned to keep protection strapped to him at all times, his piece at the crib for now because the party. Having already put out his first mixtape, he was what mainstream viewed as a threat. A true menace to society.

"Throw me some slack, dog," said J-Play.

Junior tripped between strides. He caught himself, saying, "Whoa."

The girls, the scene, the money—some he and his partner even managed to stash in their pockets. He was still thinking about the party.

As the two neared the end of the trail, E-Dog spat at the ground, nearly hitting his shoes. He had on blue Chucks Taylor's. Of course Play did too. High Tops.

Dog was a Crip by choice so it was important for Play to blend in around him. Play was anti-gang related.

"I 'gotta drain the weasel, dog," J-Play said as they approached the end of the trail. J-Play went to the end of the pavement and worked himself inside the bushes and proceeded to handle his business.

"You 'gone make them dead 'homies drink yo piss?"

E-Dog asked. "That's foul motherfucka."

But J-Play just went to whistling a slight tune. Something like: "*Rrr, reo, whh…, rrwwh...*"

Everybody in Raw Hills with a nickname had earned it. And like E-Dog, J-Play earned his nickname last year in the tenth grade. He gained a respectful reputation playing baseball. He had been carved out at a young age to be a fine player with his dad putting him in little league as a youth.

Even so it wasn't until the last three games of the season when the coach finally put him in as a regular behind the plate. Playing catcher on defense gave him an early feel for the game. As a result he blasted 13 RBI's in the final games, capping the year off with a soaring .489 Batting Average. The people of Eastern L.A. began to call him J-Play because, more often than not, he put the ball into play. He particularly looked up to the brothers in the Major League like Jason Heyward. Yet there are no Black catchers in the game so he modeled his game after Jorge' Posada, a switch hitter like him. Entering his junior season, Play was viewed as an exception to the rules. A Black catcher on an otherwise all white team.

The fruits of his labor were starting to pay off. Bombarded with too many scholarships he was ready to commit to USC on a full ride. He just had to come. Go Trojans.

Meanwhile, the Dog just could not get over what his homie had said. "Where do you think are homie?"

Play tried to hold his focus as an outline of a body formed in the debris.

E-Dog was rude because he gave J no privacy while he tried to take care of his business.

"But for real though. The west coast is different," he said. "Maybe if this was Atlanta or some shit you could say 'something like that. Shid, you could say whatever you want then—"

"You a grammar expert now, dog?"

E-Dog continued to give Junior the business. He made a *L* with his left hand and an *A* with his right hand then put them together, the L halfway above the A, forming *LA*. "This LA Shid!"

E-Dog rambled on. "And you've been living here how long now? Three Years? I don't know, maybe the big city ain't for you?"

"All right, all right," J-Play said as he zipped up his pants and fought his way back on the trail. "God damn, dog."

J had had about enough. And E-Dog tone had increased. Real talk. E-Dog needed to cool down, at least until they made it out of the trail. What if some fools heard them?

But E was on a roll now. He could not stop blasting his partner. E-Dog loved to talk shit.

"If this was Compton, you might've had 'yo big narrow ass shot. Them nigga's made a nigga feel silly out this 'motherfucka."

While urinating, Junior noticed a bomb lying peacefully asleep. No homo or anything. But the bomb appeared to be in sync. Junior figured he was dreaming or some shit. He started to tell E but declined. Figured he'd do something stupid or elementary like he always ended up doing.

"This the '*Land of Sipping on Jin and Juice*'," E-Dog explained, more or less preaching. His enthusiasm faded, letting the situation go. Lights could now be seen toward the crossing exit. Alas, they were at the end of the trail.

Junior took out a wad of bills and flashed them in the air. "Look at all this money though nigga."

A couple twenty dollar bills dropped on the ground beneath him. Junior took to sweeping his mess. E-Dog smirked, as if saying, "That's all the money you got?"

In the dividing light at the edge of the trail someone was whistling out an unfamiliar tune: "Whreoo..ryy..."

"You heard that?" In a split second, E-Dog's demeanor suddenly took a 180 degree turn.

Junior opened his mouth to answer but the words never made it out.

"Break Yo Self FOOL!" shouted a voice.

"Don't Move or I'll bust a cap in Yo' Ass!" shouted another man dressed in all black attire with a black hat and Gucci bandana covering his nose and mouth. Pointing an assault rifle at either boy.

E-Dog noted he had on standard black and white Chuck Taylor's. Neither a Blood nor Crip—a Folk.

"Give Me what you got!!"

Junior managed to shove the wad of stacks back in his jeans but those two twenty's dollar bills remained on the trail's floor. Are these nigga's working together or by themselves? Junior wondered.

"Fuck! Not a stickup!" E-Dog painfully said.

Junior managed to get a good glance up at the man in dark shades after putting both hands on his head like a police arrest. The man had on raggedy clothes and he looked familiar, even recent. Was he at the party? No. J-Play had not seen him there. Then he remembered. He looked like the bomb lying fast asleep!

"Why don't yawl fools go ahead and leave us alone?" E-Dog suggested. "We broke. We ain't got shit." The Dog then asked, "And homie, don't I know you Folk? From Decadence Studio?"

Real recognize real.

"JUST SHUT THE FUCK UP! And Empty Them *Motherfucking* Pockets!" said the man with the bandana.

"I'll give yawl whatever, but don't do anything you'd regret!" Junior blindly attempted negotiation.

"Probably been following us the whole time or some shit." Dog said. "Crept up on us smooth. Like a drive by. Don't yawl got nothing better to do? Man these busters ain't fixing to do nothing. Better hurry up and let us be for I—"

The stick up men cut him off: "Shut. The Fuck. Up!"

One of the men with guns looked down at the ground. And at that moment, everybody else looked down and saw the green bills of money. It was two twenty dollar bills on the ground.

Dumbfounded, Junior and E-Dog glimpsed at each other. Then the two boys took off at full speed, E-Dog a yard on Junior.

Suddenly the situation became serious. Automatic fingers locked up and banana clips let loose. Gunshots were fired and pitiful screams could be heard from a mile away.

Sagging, with pants hanging half off his ass, E-Dog tripped and fell to the ground. But J-Play kept running. And so did the bullets. "AHHW!"

Out of the shagginess of the trail into the city of Los Angeles that swallowed its prey like an early bird in the morning, an Amazon of African American descent song out:

"Let peace be in our cities!"

The gang bangers scrambled for it. The one J-Play thought was a bomb ran to him, though, and short-changed his pockets. While he did so, the robber saw E-Dog raise out of the Raw Hills fence. "Punk Ass nigga!" he feigned.

Bootlegged style, the gang bangers attention was caught. The boy on the ground resembled the local base-ball phenom. He would tell his partner but he'd just talk denial talk.

The motherfucking Dog scrambled to his feet, out of the trails, and dashed to his crib to get his automatic, knowing his best friend was dead. Plagued with rage, he grabbed his pistol and flew out the door.

Revenge was now or never.

AVOID THEM ALL

—

My hat is on as it was supposed to be, fitted on the top of my head. I adjust my dingy shirt pocket, checking to make sure I have a few hooks to spare just in case. Check. I do. I stroke the water below and sail off into the Hillsborough River in my canoe, forming baby ripples as my paddle becomes one with the morning bracket water. My fishing spot is right up yonder. It is surrounded by lily pads, teeming bushes, and green foliage of summer. I settle my mini canoe around the bubbles in the area, brush the boat against a bush, and begin to work up a line for Black Crappie appeal. My tackle box is old and junky as is the inside of my boat. Nonetheless, I find the bait I caught earlier: some tadpoles under a pile of sunflower seeds. The sun is bright but my hope is even brighter.

I set a good-sized tadpole onto the hook of my fishing rod, which so happens to be a Shakespeare *Tiger* that I stole from my dad a while ago. Knowing him, he hasn't noticed it missing. Fishing was never a pleasure of his because he was caught up in the fast life. Me, I always liked fishing. Not only is it peaceful, but I am good at it, and I always had something to fall back on whenever I got hungry. Like right now.

"Droop!" The water ripples a big splash when I drop my line down in the bubbling school of speckled perch.

There is a State Park right around the corner and I am careful not to make noise so I won't attract attention from the fishermen or whoever else is on the dock. I do not want anyone to catch me by myself, because they'd get suspicious. Mainly, the law is what I am trying to avoid.

I slide my Aviator shades on and watch my orange cork dance around, carefully comparing its movements from the water's natural flow to what could be the tug of a fish.

Strike One! The cork quickly jolts down under water. I have a pocket of time in which I must snatch the line upward, and then hook, line, and sink her. It always happens so fast but I am sharp today and I time it and bring up a big fat slab! This speck is big enough to be breakfast by itself. Overjoyed, I snatch it off the hook and survey its beauty as a fish and creature of nature. I could sell it for an easy 10 bucks but I won't. Specks are usually caught during winter, when the water is icy and relatively high. However if you have a boat that can navigate you into deep water, you can test your luck where they really are.

As I empty the fish into my bucket, it makes a couple whips and splashes with its powerful body that is loud enough to awaken the dead. I catch two more in the span of 15 minutes. I place them in the bucket with the first one and return to the water. By this time, I have made a lot of noise in the area. Three fishes are in the bucket. I have enough to last me all day today. But I will to try to catch another fish before I go. This is my kind of fishing.

While I am reeling in the line, the shrubs nearby began shaking. A Fishing Game woman appears from the bushes. She is short and stocky. Placing both hands on her hips, she then smiles. Smiles!

"Any luck yet, kid?" she asks me.

I lay the fishing pole on the boat, securing it for take-off. "I haven't got a bite." I lie, trying to sound as grown up as possible and hoping that trouble here will let me go. "I was just packing it up for the morning. I hate to come home empty handed but I have no choice."

As I say this, the Game woman comes as close as she can without falling over the bay she is standing on.

"Up yonder on the deck they are having some luck," she bribes. "They've caught a few mullet."

"Oh, for real?" I reply as I sit down with my paddle in hand. She could be totally bullshitting me. I know that there are people who catch mullet in this park—but I don't have the proper tackle to catch mullet by boat. It's time for me to leave anyways. "I believe you. But I must leave now."

"All right. How old are you kid?"

Finally, she asks me. I am old enough to be in a boat by myself so I am old enough to have a fishing license. Luckily for me, my canoe is halfway down the river when she asked me, so she has no chance of catching me.

"I am old enough to mind my own business," I say, almost out of her eyesight. I turn on the radio inside my boat and sing the lyrics aloud. "What you know about this?" I taunt.

"Pretty boy swag—who dat El Debarge?"

She was way off.

"Wrong. Soulja boy."

I like her, even though she was obviously stuck in her day with old school music that my mother listens to. I can't even lie though. I took a liking to many of the "good bands" through hearing my mom play artists like The Isley

Brothers, The Commodores, and Michael Jackson.

The bay from the swamp is up ahead and the trees shade me from the sunlight. I turn the radio off.

As I bring the canoe up onto land, I look down at my legs, and then into my face using the reflection of the water. While I was growing up, my family always told me I had African legs. Inspecting myself, I can see why.

My legs are black and strong, like an African coming from netting a sack full of piranhas. My face is ashy with a hint of purple, thanks to the sun's glare. In school, whenever clowns joked on me with African name-calling, I pictured a lost slave running away from his master, running to freedom.

I pull myself from my trance and hide my boat in the abandoned farm house surrounded by plants and weeds.

In my reflection I saw an older me with nappy hair starting to appear along my cheeks and face. The Fishing Game Warden hadn't recognized me. In the last two months, I've grown from a boy to a man. Maybe this is why the Fishing Game woman hadn't recognized me.

I relieve myself in the farm house. My cooking dishes and clothes are also hidden in here. I grab a hat and place it far back on my head. I put on some flip-flops. I grab my wallet and to the local Wal-Mart store I go. I am in need of a can of Castrol oil to fry my fish.

While walking to the store I pass a bus terminal. I watch crows scoop up crumbs and people of all ilk. Surviving on my own since I ran away from home is giving me that *Tom Sawyer* feel—free and adventurous, like a young man my age should be.

The day I left my house was the last day I saw my mother. She was curled up Indian style, reading scriptures

from the Bible. The day before had been a storm. My dad
had taken to beating her up again. He had come home
from work angry and frustrated because his job had told
him to take next week off. I heard him ramp and rage at
my mom, and then slap her with his back hand. At the
time, I was playing "NBA Live 2011." When I heard my
mom in pain, I went out to see my dad standing over her.
I intervened, pushed him back, and asked mom if she was
all right.

I always wondered why he never went fishing on his
days off.

Escalate was all it did from there. I guarded my Mom
as my Dad started to fuss and wildly rage at me saying,
"You don't do shit here boy! You don't pay any bills! I put
you into this world, and I'll you take out!"

I held my ground. Otherwise, he'd keep beating my
mom until she got bruises and was unable to come out in
public, frightened that her neighbors would see her. The
next thing I knew, my dad charged me and we were on the
ground in front of the house rolling with each other,
throwing bows.

"Tate! Tate!" screamed my mother. I couldn't tell
which one of us she was yelling at since I was Tate Junior.
My father is Tate Senior.

It never felt like it, though. I never felt close to my
dad. We never shared that bond that I see so often between other fathers and son tandems fishing together.
Probably why it was so easy for us to squabble. He felt like
another nigga on the streets. All he cared about was money. All he wanted was more of it.

When the fight ended, my dad cursed up a cycle and
grabbed items I cannot recall, and said to me, "I don't

want to see you back in my house! You hear, Boy?"

Then he left, just left. None of us was seriously in-jured from fighting in front of our house. Our reputation was damaged, though, as our nosy neighbors watched on like backward owls.

It remains a mystery how it never stormed that day.

As I enter Wal-Mart, I can honestly say that I don't miss anything from home. Not even my X-Box 360. We lived in a three-room house where I was the only child but by my father had kids from other women.

I lied. There is one thing I miss: Chief. That's my pet dog. I named him after my favorite NFL team, The Kan-sas City Chiefs. I wonder if my mom has been feeding him properly. With me gone for almost 2 months, surely she'd noticed the barking and kept him fed to hush up. Feeding the dog was the only chore I had around the house so it was the only way which my absence would be felt.

That and eat. Often, the only reason I saw my mom was when I came out of my room to eat.

I find the fish ingredients on the far isle and cuff the oil while going to the front of the store. There are eight or nine checkout isles open and all of them are packed. This is typical for Wal-Mart. Wal-Mart swear they are so up on their security when they are not. Their business makes them vulnerable. I go under a closed register, and hide the item under my shirt. Then out the store I go. Stealing from Wal-Mart is easy as cake.

There are more cars in the parking lot than when I came in. Wal-Mart has to be a *monopoly*. I start walking back to the farm house. Before I ran away, I had been applying for jobs. Now I no longer wanted to apply to Wal-Mart. Rather a more laid back store. Perhaps Winn-

Dixie or somewhere.

In the store, I saw Marlin, my neighbor, before I left home. I turned the other way when I saw him so that he would not recognize me. I don't think he saw my dad and I fight, but surely he has noticed my absence from the house by now.

We went to the same school. In a couple of weeks, we're supposed to start school. Last year I had Marlin in a few classes. The day I ran away from home was the third to last day of school. I had missed all of my final exams but still managed to pass my classes. I kept my grades high, so when it came time for Finals it didn't matter if I passed them or not. In fact, some of my teachers told me I didn't have to take their finals because I'd still pass the class.

Therefore with this school year approaching I will have to make a decision. Will I go to school and return home or remain like this? I could remain a runaway until April, at least, when income tax time is over. You can't file for a child who is a runaway. That would serve my dad well for the things he'd done. I learned this from Ms. Beusy, my Economics teacher. She was getting a divorce during the school year and would always tell her class that we helped her get through it.

Hopefully, she could talk to my mom about getting a divorce.

I reach my spot at the farm house and start making breakfast. Ms. Beusy's Economics class has served me well for the last two months. Saving resources, eating on a plan and taking care of me were all things I learned from her class that helped me to survive on my own.

I fry the fish on the fryer after making a fire from

matches and lighter fluid. After this, I make some grits, chop a cucumber, and eat.

When I finish, I clean my canoe from the river's dirt. Then I place it inside the farm, hidden from any happy camper who may come inside the farmhouse. Thinking of home, I dress quickly and throw on some of my good clothes. I need to check on Chief and my mother.

While walking, I look over myself and think. This year, I probably won't get any school clothes. I am a runaway. What should I expect?

The clothes that I have on are from last school year but they are still fresh and I note my swagger as I walk. I have on a pair of *Bape and Apes* with snakeskin on the star emblem. I have a New York Knick's cap on. I wear brown cargo pants that match my black Ralph Lauren T-shirt. I am in full chick magnetic mode. It would be hard to guess I was homeless.

When I enter my neighborhood, many memories began to surface. I remember the basketball games me and my friends use to play around this time of the year. Ripping and running. There is nothing like drinking an ice cold glass of water after a hot game of basketball!

I grew up in this neighborhood all my life. I watched neighbors come and go. In some cases, they would go and then come right back again. One thing that I could say about my father is that he was dependable. He provided for his family and kept a roof over our heads. I have seen households come crashing down due to the laziness of the man of the house. My dad could never be one of those.

Maybe his ambition and obsession over money was not such a bad thing. Maybe I should count my blessings. Then again, if he just kept his hands off my mother...

As I make a turnout of someone's driveway, I hear yelling and turn to see people arguing and angrily pointing from their grass to me. They are not speaking English. So I politely turn my head away and keep going. Like I care.

If I can recall, the Flip Lady used to stay in that house.

My house is right up ahead if I cross the front of our neighbor's backyard. But I won't do that because if someone is home, the person will easily spot me. So I walk on the sidewalk. As I do, a mailman comes and stops at the mail box.

My mom car is parked in the driveway but my dad truck is gone. When I reach our driveway, Marlin suddenly finds me. Darn!

He calls out: "I heard about your dad, Tate. I'm sorry for your loss."

"What?" I pardon.

"Your dad," Marlin appears from his house and comes over to me. "I heard he joined Alcoholics Anonymous. He needs professional help."

I look Marlin up and down. Like me, he has grown some over the summer and has facial hair. "When did you hear this?" I ask.

"About a week ago," Marlin says. "I wish your family luck. We keep you all in our prayers at my house. Can you believe our senior year came so fast? It's right around the corner?" He turns and walks out the same way I came in.

He didn't mention the fight or the fact that I had run away for virtually two months. It was a chance that he didn't know. However, he surely had heard of the fight by now from the neighbors.

As I walk to the side of the house, I pull out the sack

of bones that I brought for Chief. He begins to bark before he can even see me. "Roof, Roof!" A half bark, half cry.

"Orite Dawg." Chief greets me with a curtsy bow and I pet him on his head like he likes it. "You've been a good boy?"

I empty the bones into his dog bowl. He attacks them until there are none left. Chief has been hungry indeed.

I put fresh water in his drinking bucket and try not to make noise.

Afterward, I tip toe toward the patio door to peek in. A woman inside has her back turned to me reading a book. It is my mother!

She is hunched over a wooden chair that's connected to the dining room table. Her hair is in a ponytail smoother than a stallions hide. Her skin is creamy and this matches the wife beater and blouse she wears. My mother is a beautiful woman.

I look harder and see that the book she is reading is *The Things That Keep us Here* by Carla Buckley. I smile because I had recommended that she read this novel after I had read it and was stunned by its reality of an epidemic that could happen on Earth. This was the last book I read before running away.

What Marlin told me must be true. My mother finally gave my dad an alternative to dealing with his anger. She made him go to rehab.

To me, AA stands for "Angry Assholes."

Chief begins barking, suspicious of what I am doing at the patio. My mom starts to turn around and I tap twice on the patio window before she sees me. I jolt away from the patio door. I run up toward our neighbor's back yard and then sprint from the house.

I think my mom saw my feet when I went. She knew it was me. She recognized the taps on the window. This is what I wanted—for her to know I was all right. I didn't want her to worry.

My mother always knew that I was never a talker.

As I leave the neighborhood, I a car sitting on 21-inch rims passes me. The driver has gold teeth. Music blasting from powerful speakers. A song from Eminem's *Recovery* album is playing. This is the last album I bought from the store before running away.

Going back to the farmhouse, I find it silly that I have been hiding out for no reason with my dad gone. I have been dodging people and afraid to live life because of what? I should have gone home by now. This same fear hinders me in life—waiting to do things—scared of the consequences. I never tell anyone about it but it's just there. It is something my parents raised me up in: Latent fear. Being subconsciously afraid of failure and what success may bring.

Maybe this is the same fear my dad felt. Maybe.

It took me ten minutes to reach the farm-house. When I get there, I feel something is different. A pearl colored rabbit leaps over my sneakers. Yesterday that rabbit would have been lunch. Not anymore

I find a sack of my clothes and dishes on the grass. "Shoot," I say to myself. When I enter the farm-house, two men are eying the place and inspecting.

"Why are you guys here for?" I question.

"We're inspecting it. What's it look like? It's a good chance we buy it out."

Walking out of the farm house, I decide to lose my

canoe. I slide my canoe on top of the river and watch it sink in the deep Hillsborough River. It descends into the depths of the water. My radio and sunflower seeds sink along with it. I grab the rest of my stuff from the ground and head out.

I have school to get ready for in the fall.

FIRST THINGS FIRST

—

One morning, the phone rang. I was coming out the shower when the ring's screeched throughout my crib. I wiped myself down and tied the lush towel around my waist and went downstairs to my customized office. Sensing business, I wanted to answer this phone call.

"Jeremiah the phone is ringing!" Hannah, my latest bedroom victim, yelled out. She was scrambling eggs, and the meal in the making smelled like something to look forward to.

I mark out, "I'm on my way." Nearing the end of the flight of stairs, beads of water drip off of my physique.

"Once you answer the phone, breakfast will be ready!" she called out. "This is my recipe that I only cook for guys I like—eggs, sausage, and toast, with cheese."

"Roger that," I said, glad to know she is finding her way around my place so well. My one night stand is finding the right food and the whole nine. She is quite comfortable for a guy she just met in the last 24 hours.

As I cascade into my self-made office, the phone yelping grow louder and the sun hits me through my blinds as I sit in my office chair. As I pick the phone up off the receiver, I hear Hannah asking, "Where's the vegetable oil?"

I found it funny that Hannah—nationally televised

Chef—is now in my kitchen cooking up a dish. Last night, after an "after party", I had set my eyes on the shapely chef and knew I had to have her. White girl or not.

Judging that only a few more rings were left, I move in a hurry to raise the phone to my ear. "Hello?" I answered.

"Jeremiah! We need to talk. And now kid." It is an urgent and shaken tone of a familiar voice.

"Bill!" Bill is my account manager, my everything, at least financial wise. I had guessed right: Business it was!

"Look kid. I need you to listen up and I need you to focus," Bill ordered.

Bills voice sounded crucial and his tone was straight forward. Something was up. Something was up indeed.

I smoothen out the framed glass pictures of horses and Nascar memories. I never fail to reflect on all those risky bets I risked which would become winners. Jeff Gordon and I shook hands in front of his car in the midst of a ribbon and glitter shower after he finished #1 at the *Daytona 500*. This photograph, a favorite, is placed on the top of my laptop. Every time I see it, I get purple chills because on that summer day, I took the underdog in Gordon over the more favored Jimmie Johnson. But I, I, the risk taker, was the one who came out with 600K!

I put the phone close to my ear and said, "All ears Bill."

Bill breathed in a big sigh.

"All right Jeremiah. I want you to listen and listen well. There is no good way to say this so I am just going to say it. Around eight this morning, three hours ago, someone got into all of your accounts, somehow with your identity. Under your name, they made numerous withdrawals from all of your accounts until they wiped them clean. I know it wasn't you because it was done all at once. In other words, a team job. The bank was late recognizing this scandal and by then it was too late. Jeremiah you're bankrupt."

I remove the phone from my ear and sink back in my luxury seat. Bill, my accountant, wanted to know what I had to say, but I was speechless.

"Jeremiah... Jeremiah?" he blurted. "Are we still there?"

"Yeah..." I could feel myself becoming numb.

I heard Hannah yelling, "Jeremiah, where is the vegetable oil at boo?" Her voice sounded closer now. "You know I can't whip anything up without oil. No vegetable oil, no meal."

Bill cleared his throat on the other end of the line. "Jeremiah. This is the part where I need you to focus. If you don't believe me, you can check your accounts for yourself but I there all empty. Me and your banks are seriously looking at a series of electronic activities linking your accounts to a number of illegal withdrawals. Jeremiah, we can still get your money back if we crack some codes."

I took a deep breath, making a sigh that was barely audible. The star status phone was barely clinched in my grasp. Lazering in on the creatively office with its futuristic styles, I take a look into the window to see the setting of another summer's day.

Drowning in disbelief, I hold the phone up. "How could this be? I need the plan for how you are going to get my money back, or else you're fired Bill! I am bankrupt! Bankrupt, Bill! Penniless! All that money I'm worth!"

I was yelling now. "How can I explain bankrupt to

the Gambling casino? I'm one of the wealthier gamblers in the club!"

Hannah, the Chef, must have found the vegetable oil by now. She had stopped her yelling. And maybe she was making another dish or two. I sure hadn't heard her in a while.

Through the tense reception I could hear a bead of sweat drop from Bills bald head. "Please, don't make assumptions without information Jeremiah. Mind you that you are broke and if you don't get paid, I don't get paid either. If we maintain communication, we can work together to catch these morons and get your money back—"

I heard a noise from somewhere—close to outside—I couldn't tell. And then suddenly the line went blank. That was the last I heard from my accountant. Bill was gone, the communication had somehow been deadened.

My sixth sense felt a movement from behind where the elegant dining room was. I turned to see a perturbed Hannah, mouth open, with one of my cooking forks in her hand.

"You're Bankrupt?" she asked.

"Hannah? I didn't know you were listening."

The stainless fork dropped to the ground and her expression became ugly. "Please, tell me you're not bankrupt?"

"Hannah, do not worry," I say trying to calm her down, which is very hard to do when your mind is racing. "Pretend like you didn't hear anything and finish breakfast."

Go back to the kitchen and finish cooking. Because.

"Jeremiah. I'm sorry. But I can't be with a penniless man. I can't have anyone know I slept with a broke bum.

Goodbye Jeremiah. And good luck."

And just like that she left. I heard her pack some clothes and shortly after the front door opened and her Convertible engine ignite. The sausage was still frying.

"You were only a one night stand anyway, White Bitch!" I wanted to yell from out the window. But what lay ahead of me was more important. My money.

The phone didn't shut off by itself. I check the phone outlet power and find the plug is still attached. Odd. Did the power stop flowing in my house altogether? Then I checked the laptop. It too is powerless. I go down stairs and into the kitchen to find the oven on and the sausage burning to crisp. I turn the oven off and take the pan of sausage off the burner.

What in the world? If anything, this was strange. The oven power was working but the cable and internet connection had gone dead. How could this be? Impossible. It couldn't be possible.

Unless there was something I didn't know.

Bankruptcy. The very thought of being bankrupt sent shivers up my spine. All the bets and risks and chances that I had taken to get this point—the gambling Casino, my plaques, my Nascar trophies, and winning races: all of which were on display in the living room—had just been snatched away from me. And if I didn't act quickly and get Bill back on the line, it may be gone forever!

Before the line went dead I remember Bill saying, "'If we stay on the line we may be able to track down the bad guys to get your money back...'"

I run a 23 year old hand through my fade. The man I trusted most told me that I am about to lose every dollar I had worked for. The feeling was deadly.

I thought back to remember if there was anyone I knew who could have found my identity in their hands. None crossed my mind.

Suddenly, an obvious answer struck me. Hannah! She was the only one who could have snuck in my place and her abrupt behavior made her all more liable. But Hannah was a millionaire of her own. In fact, she had more money than I did. Easily. I started to go up to my master's office to check my superb surveillance camera system. But Hannah did not fit this description. There was no way she could be involved in this scandal.

Then who was it then?

Closing my eyes and leaning on the kitchen wall, I recall when the phone went dead. It didn't just static out or loose connection. The phone line had completely been shut off during our tense call.

I had paid my cable bill last time I checked so unless Bright House was checking for bootleg cable, there could only be one other answer: Someone outside had cut my cable line! Remembering my brand new cell phone in my room, silly me, I start up the stairs in a frantic effort. I had to get Bill, my accountant back on the phone and very soon. Or else!

But as I took the first 3 steps from the flight of stairs, something out of the corner of my eye caused me to freeze in my traps. Someone in all black darted pass my patio door, moving very fast. I knew what I saw and cable men didn't dress like this.

Someone out there was trying to end my means of communication!

I quickly step from the stairs and onto the ground floor. I peek out the patio door but see nothing.

I quietly slip out the house, but not before picking up the fork that Hannah dropped in my office, and sliding on a pair of basketball shorts. I tip around the garage and onto the side of the house where the phone cables are installed. The knife is tight in my palm.

"Phipaff!" suddenly a loud sound ejects from the ground.

"Fuck!" I hear a deep voice groan.

Not wanting to wait to become a victim (even though I kind of already was), I hurriedly circled to the back yard where a man dressed in all black mugging clothes is lying on his stomach. A wire cutter lay in the grass where he tripped.

"Who in the *Clown's World* are you and why did you cut my cable? Don't you know that's a lawsuit?" I would show no mercy to this clown. That's all he was, anyway. A bozo.

I stomp my feet in his back and wave the knife in the air.

"Don't ask me," the powerless man said. "I was just walking by when some people gave me that tool and told me to cut the cable to this house. They said they'd watch and if I did it, I would get four grand."

Four Grand. They, whoever they were, were offering him crumbs from a feast. It sounded about right.

"Who is they?"

"I don't know some filthy Indian bunch. They were riding in a Suburban."

"Did they tell you their motives behind doing this? Like why they would cut someone's cable in broad daylight?"

"No, nothing like that." The bandits back squirmed

beneath my foot. "Can you take your feet off my back? It's hot enough as it is."

I put the knife to his throat to make myself clear. "I've never seen you around here. This neighborhood is top flight security. Waking up today, I found out that I've just fallen bankrupt to the hands of identity theft. Then this. I find some guy who doesn't belong in my neighborhood has cut the line to my cable and phone line. I need answers."

He said, "Alright, but you have to let me go, cool?"

I wanted to laugh. But instead I said, "Never leave a visitors house until you're dismissed. Thats rude. Now tell me who sent you."

"Well up until today my track record with Looby's, a major systems programmer that does dirty jobs for dirtier people, was the best in the business so we hopped over here to do a new job," he revealed. "So if you want the actual people, I won't know. You'll have to ask the owner of Looby's."

I yanked him up by the ear. This was my money we were talking about at stake! All the work I had put in to obtain my wealth...I was not ready to watch it flee. I needed to get to my cell phone.

"How about you call this place—I have a phone for you. You said you were working with a team, right? We will frame them then catch them. Afterward, you can sit in my office and you will come up with a plan to get my money back. Try anything clever and I'm buzzing for the cops. Bet that! I hope you enjoy eating very, very crispy sausage too."

STRIP CLUB SHAWTY

—

A L.A. Laker game beamed bright from the television box up in the ceiling. Other than the small light from the bar, and jewelry on many of the men's wrist, the T.V. was the only source of light on the whole floor.

"At a Boy!" One of the men sitting solo among the bar shouted up at the cable box. Living in Florida, he barely got to see his favorite NBA team play. Different time zones conflicted. When he could, he tried not to miss the Laker's play. If he had to go to a strip club to see them— so be it. And this game they proved not to upset him.

"That's what I'm talking about, Baby!" He yelled as he rose to his feet in joy. Kobe Bryant just hit a game winning buzzer beater to win the game! Joy!

The man name was King.

It was past midnight. Many of the regulars were starting to feel the alcohol soak into their bloodstreams, unlike the stragglers who skipped drinks since they missed the "Everyone Drinks Free Till' Midnight" freebie.

The night was just getting started.

King shifted his weight to get off the stool. His long john coat drooped down, covering his cop uniform.

He slowly walked through the main room into the center doors where men were seated at small tables. On a table, a stripper was seductively dancing. She was pleasing her fans who loved every bit of the act before them. About twenty five circular tables were all seated with four men or more, each table with a stripper on it.

This room was where the main phase bar was. King hovered over to the bar stools. On the way he got paper cut—"Ouch!"—with cash dollar bills raining down from above.

King heard a man say, "Boy if she keeps shaking it like that I might go throwing hundreds!"

"Toast to that Brother!" said another man with a marriage ring on his finger. "Down south in Miami that's all they throw at King of Diamonds."

Tired and slouching, King ordered a drink.

"Would you like a lemon slice on the side?" the waiter asked.

"No," King managed to squeeze out.

"That's fine. Give me a few, will you." The waiter (who told King to call her Nea) briskly walked to the beverage filters and vigorously filled a tall glass halfway with ice. She held it under an adjacent filter and poured a gold liquid into the glass, filling it up.

Alcohol bubbles spilled on the bar as she slid the drink to the half dozed man sitting on the stool. "There you are sir. Your total is $8.75." she said.

King looked inside the drink. "This the strongest stuff you got, right?"

"Chamberlagne Crystal. Sixty percent alcohol," Nea said. "Finest in the state."

King handed her the money. He grabbed the tall glass with his flat right hand and brought it to his mouth. He drunk long enough to have camel's back.

When he was through, he put the glass on the bar

with a "Thud!" He opened his eyes and saw Nea walking away from him.

"Damn Girl!" The booze was already starting to work its way into King's blood stream. But seriously, he hadn't noticed the bartender's shapely figure before. Nea had it "going on".

Another heavy set man came pouring in and seated himself on the bar to the left of King.

"Hey Nea, over here," the heavyset man called. "Let's talk. And then I want a cold one."

King turned his head to the man. He did a quick look down of him, and as he did so he gave a suck of his teeth: "Ckwjj."

The first thing King noticed was he was white. And he was big, very big. King also liked the Nike's he wore: they were fresh.

When King sucked his teeth, the man scratched his head and said, "What the Fuck?"

"Coming Black," Nea the waitress called out, heading towards him.

"Black?" King said aloud. Was his mind playing tricks on him? Was the Crystal drink impairing his hearing?

Then he put two plus two together. The shoes. The Dialogue. Black, the name. The man must be a local. He also came to the strip lounge a lot. This was probably how he knew Nea. And, above all, he thought he was a black man.

King coughed. Before Nea could get to Mr. Black, he grabbed her by the arm. "Damn you looking good girl. Way too good."

"What the Fuck?" Black said. His face looked confused.

Nea shot her free arm in the air, the one that she used as a notepad for orders. "What are you doing?" she asked King. Then to Black: "Black, don't trip. I don't even know this guy."

From behind them, to King's back, the door opened, gracing the strip club with light. With this quick eclipse of light, King was able to see that this "Black" character had tattoos all over his neck and forearms from what he could judge. King let the bartender loose. "Are you serious about this guy? He's not even Black."

Nea stumbled from his release. She walked to where Black was now standing and said, "I'm as serious as I want to be."

King saw that "Black" was now standing. King turned the other way as Nea leaned over the counter and kissed Mr. Black.

King coughed.

"What the Fuck?" Black asked again. Black beamed at King, like he dared this black guy to try to get at his girl.

Nea leaned on the counter and tried to calm him down. "Black, baby chill," she said. "C'mon, let's talk."

Suddenly King jumped up. A lose $100 dollar bill grazed the side of his head. The feeling brought him into full attention. He swung his palm at the bill and stumped it with his work boots. "So the girls on the strip poles had the men up to 100's now," King thought.

King rose from the bar, making a torturous noise. While he was at it, he let out a fart. Then he checked his Rolex. It was almost one o'clock at night and it was time for King to be heading home. He had work to get to in the afternoon and didn't want to have his wife worried. The kids should be asleep.

"Outee." King walked from the bar to the stripper tables and past the lines of television sets. The "EXIT" door was after the main strippers stand. Wasted, he walked pass the concentrated area of lustful men. King was suddenly approached by two security guard's.

"Sir, where do you think you're going?" one of them said, arms folded.

"The show is right here," said the other, pointing to the half-naked stripper on the stage.

King looked up. The stripper was upside down on the pole with her legs wrapped around it. This position made her look as if she were an anaconda wrapped around a tree ready to pounce on its prey.

"I'm too drunk to be tired and too tired to be drunk," King admitted. "That's how I feel right now."

"Go Vanilla! Go!" The men nearest the stripper shouted. King saw a bunch of dollar bills that surrounded the pole, adding to the environment. Call it compost.

"I was leaving," King said.

King shoved his way into a crowd of people, relieved to be away from the guards. Their breaths were kicking.

King walked to the exit doors and as he did so a familiar looking woman was approaching from the main pole above. King grabbed the door handle and was about to open it when he heard a close voice. "How was I?" It was a female voice.

King stopped. "Vanilla?" The stripper stood above him with a load of dollar bills in her hand. It looked like enough money to pay his mortgage this month.

"What are you deaf?" she asked, counting.

"No. You were great," King replied. Within such a close vicinity to the physically gifted Vanilla, he now understood why she had this stripper name. Baby's skin was soft and creamy which made her complexion standout with her golden hair. Everything on her body—curves, waist, and panty line—gave King the impression that she tasted like ice pure vanilla.

"They should call you Extra Vanilla instead," he said.

The naked stripper laughed at his comment. "I like your style. Here's a hundred for sportsmanship."

She flipped a bill at King. As she did, her left breast popped out. King let the bill float away.

Vanilla then asked, "Where were you going? That's not an exit."

King looked up and around. "Excuse me but it says EXIT." King pointed toward the orange fluorescent light above the steel door.

"That an *Emergency Exit*."

"Well this is an emergency. I have to get home. And now too." King twisted the handle to the door.

"No!—" Vanilla's tone was unmistakable.

"Don't worry. I'll make it quick." He opened the door.

"You don't understand! You'll let them in!"

King opened the door wider. "Let who in?"

"BEEM!"

Suddenly a very loud burst of metal clacking with metal came from the outside of the emergency exit. The impact was so strong that it sprung the door open and King fell to the hard floor. "Hey P, The Door is OPEN!" someone shouted from outside.

King remained on the ground as three raggedy goons entered through.

"NO!" Vanilla exalted.

The first to enter had a .45 caliber pistol in his hand. He stepped over King then looked at Vanilla.

"Don't you thugs come here causing no trouble like y'all did last time!"

Vanilla was pleading!

The second of the goons who entered side stepped King and tried to grab Vanilla by the thigh. "We won't bitch. As long as you promise to show us good time?"

Vanilla ran to the back of the stage. "ILL!" she yelled as she ran. "You Bastards Stink!" Before she ran, she spit down at the men beneath her.

A large portion landed on the second goon. "That Fucking Bitch!"

"Cool down, Rugs. We'll get her later," said the first goon as he tucked his gun in his hip, now hidden by a baggy white T. "Let's see if we can find Black first."

The third goon stepped over King.

It was pitch black outside. He adjusted his eyes to the dark street outlet. He saw a fat rat swiftly crawl from out a trash can that was lit with fire and surrounded by people. The rat crawled pass his shoes, stopped to nimble at his gator boots, and entered the strip club.

King shook miserably. The rat crawled its way into the club. King quickly shut the door before anything else came in. Fists banged on the opposite side of the door.

"*What the Fuck?*" King couldn't help but echo Black.

Black? Black! The three goon guys had mentioned his name. Yes, he heard them say it. Did those goons know Black? King recollected his thoughts as he rose to his feet. It was definitely possible. King needed to find them. He didn't give a shit about Black. He just didn't want anything bad to happen to Nea. Not Nea.

King crumbled back toward the crowd. It had grown.

"Isn't that old girl Nea on the pole?"

King searched for who had just asked this. King spotted the third goon who had stepped over him.

Then he instinctively looked up at the stripping scene. "What the—"

To his surprise, he saw Nea. Nea!—doing wonder flips on the main stripper pole!

The first goon, P, who King now saw was Spanish asked, "You know her?"

"I think so. I used to sell pills with her brother while back. When I would go to their house, she used to always be suspicious of what we were up to. That sure looks like her."

P, the leader, broke up the pact. "See if you can spot a big tall white guy with tattoos all over his body, eh. You remember Black, right? Split up. He should be in here somewhere, essay."

 Hearing this, the Laker's fan wasted no time. King fought his way into the crowd, bowing and shoving. He rushed up to the front and stood there, half dazed for a moment.

This was too unreal. King was so close to Nea that he could touch her. Her body was now naked and flexing like she was trying to win the Olympics. He had just met her 30 minutes ago. She seemed bright and full of charm. And now—Look at this! She had transformed! Strippers in disguise!

Without any thought, he grabbed this possessed stripper by the ankle. The men started "Booing." The dollars stopped raining.

"What do you think you're doing?" Nea demanded.

"Nea you're in trouble. Three dirty looking guys who are searching for Black. One of them said that you look familiar. Said that he knew your brother."

Nea wiggled her way loose. "What did he look like?"

"Skinny, ugly, and dirty looking."

The men shouted from behind them "Step off, *Asshole*!"

"Sounds like them." Nea allowed King to pull her down from the stage.

"Where the *Hell* you think you're going with her?" The red blooded men had come to see a show and weren't leaving without a fight.

A young man in street clothes and grabbed Nea by the forearm. "Chocolate Banes, you're not done yet!"

King had Nea's other arm. "Is that your stripper name? Chocolate Banes?"

Another man came out of nowhere and grabbed "Chocolate Banes" by the hips. "You weren't done yet, baby."

Nea turned her head to see Black with his arms wrapped around her middle body and waist. "Black."

King turned around. "Black! I was just about to ask Nea where you were." King then let go of Nea's arm. "You've got a problem, Mr. Black."

Suddenly someone shouted: "Rat!"

Whoever it was they were screaming their lungs out. "There's a Rat running around in Here!"

Then someone else screamed: "I'll! It's a fat rat! Run! It Bites!"

Before they knew it, King, Nea, and Black got avalanche by a bunch of antsy pansy men from every direction. In confusion, King grabbed this 'wanna-be "Black" by the hoodie.

"There are 3 sketchy looking goons who say they are trying to find a man named Black. They entered from their—" King pointed to the EXIT doors. "Unless there is another man in this strip club named Black, I think you should get ghost."

"Who opened the Emergency Doors?" Black demanded.

"It doesn't matter who opened 'em. What matters are the goons who are armed and searching for you—"

Nea pinched in. "He said their names are P and Rugs."

"Yeah I know P—," he said, but didn't get to finish.

"Big Fat Rat!" cried a stripper.

More screaming and pushing in the club. "It's a RAT! Everyone Run!"

Through the turmoil and raucous, King pulled Black forward. "So what's the deal Black? 'Cause I don't want Ms. Nea getting hurt."

"Those guys sale for me. They set up behind the club at nighttime and hustle my shit to any feen who need a booze. The club knows of the drug activity so they keep two guards by the Emergency Doors to keep peace. The only way they could have got in if someone opened the doors. Which leads to my question: Who the fuck opened those doors?"

"It was a mistake," King admitted. "And that doesn't explain what's up with Nea. She was on stage damn near naked!"

Black said, "Why are you telling me? I don't have anything to do with that."

"RAT!"

"As a matter of fact, where is Nea?" Black asked.

King looked to where Nea just was. "Must've got loosed in all this chaos. We'll have to find her."

Big as he was, Black struggled to hold his ground in all the turmoil. "What did you say? Shit. I can hardly see you in this club, let alone here your black ass."

Then King heard someone shout Black's name. "Black? Gorilla Black!"

"What the Fuck?"

"Black its *P*," said the voice. It sounded like the same voice that barged in the exit doors surprising King.

"P? How'd you get through the door?"

A scrawny figure with ashy clothes suddenly came into view from behind King. "Some moron opened it," he said. Then he pointed to King. "It looked a lot like him."

"Me?" choked King.

The pushing and shoving was forceful but the noise was simmering down as people made their way out.

Black walked toward the small area of the club where people were taking to get out the building. "Those guards are slipping." Black took a look at his phone. "On another note, I know you've sold everything by now. When we get outside, count it up and I will give you your cut. Got it?"

"Word. I need to find those other fools first, homes."

Suddenly, screaming and yelling echoed out from the turmoil. P turned around. Black and King saw a woman in the hold of two men, one on each side.

"Nea?"

It was her. It was Nea. The bartender/stripper. It was Nea!

"Black!" she screamed. "Get Them OFF ME!"

"Look what we found roaming around. We were

'gonna take her to the back," they said. "Take turns with her."

"What the Fuck!" Black demanded. "That's my girl!"

King recognized them as "the other two goons". In a flash, King's eyes grew wild. Without any regard to the men around him, King launched at Rugs and rocked him to the floor. Rugs body made a thud noise when it hit the ground. Painful, to say the least.

"My back!" Rugs yelled in misery.

While on the ground, King gave him his left fist to eat. Rugs closed his mouth. Blood gushed from Rugs nose. "That's what you get!" King scolded.

King rose to his feet to find P gripping a .45 and aiming it directly at him.

Black said: "Ay chill!" He took Nea by the hand. "You alright baby?"

Old girl Nea was crying. "These guys are horrible! Tell me you're not friends with them?"

The sight of a fool aiming a gun made people inside the club move even faster. Black motioned his way and Nea's free from harm. "P put that damn gun away!" Black barked. "I know OF them, Nea. Of them. That's all, baby."

As King stared into his eyes, P stuck the glock back into his hip. King thought. P had to be a mixture of several ethnicities His eyes were sharp, slanting at the end caps. Even through the blackness of the club, he could see the man's Native American features as strong as his compactly built frame. His build was short and low to the ground like a Mexican.

King wanted to shout, "The Three Amigos!" as they exited the building, now outside. King was the last in line after the third amigo.

Outside, King grabbed the one named Rugs in front of him and snapped his neck. "Snap," in one swift motion. The third goon ran for it, ducking off toward the emergency exit of the club.

Pass the doorway, King saw P draw his gun from underneath his pants. He looked at the wounded Rugs lying on the dirt and aimed at King. "I should have killed you when I had the chance!"

"No!" Black interrupted.

Black got his meaty hands on the scrawny P and that was enough for him to drop the gun. As soon as he did, King dropped kicked P in the face; the only thing P could do was collapse to the ground.

King now had a gun of his own in his hand. "And don't fucking move!" King ordered.

Pointing the gun back and forth from Black to P, King's wind breaker flew off and a dark gray bullet proof vest was revealed along with a shiny badge. "OPD!"

Black was worried. "C'mon! After all I did for you, you gone do me in like this?"

King kicked Black hard before kneeling beside him. "If I was a member of Black Panthers I might screw you over. Do yourself a favor and get out of here. I'll take care of your friends."

"Will do." And just like that Black was gone.

King grabbed handcuffs from under his belt and stapled the men's wrists together. Then he fondled with P's face like a kid. "How old are you?"

P wasn't sure if he was awakening or going to sleep. All he could see were butterflies. "Por 'que?"

"Rats Gone!" someone shouted. "Now call the police!

A man's got a gun!"

King rose to his feet, saying, "Because you look wet-back. But still not too young to be shipped back to your country."

"Ayos mios'.'Papi you coppers are no better than the rest of us, essay. Probably got a job you don't like. Probably go home to a broken family and wish you had more. Essay, you just like us."

"Indeed," King said, going over to where Nea stood, covering herself with his windbreaker.

"You know you should put some clothes on. You'll catch a cold like that."

Nea blushed. "I know. I wanted to thank you before I go. I appreciate everything."

"No problem. Nea, why didn't you just tell me you were a stripper?"

"Because King. It's hard enough meeting a guy as it is." Her tone was serious. "When most men find out I'm a stripper its over as far as relationships go."

"Yeah, I can relate. When someone finds out I'm a cop, I notice their moods changes on me."

In the street light, King finally got to see the real view of Nea's body line. She had definition alright. Baby's body had vocabulary. "You don't have to worry about me. I'm married with kids."

"I know." Nea planted a kiss on King's lips.

King couldn't deny something was there. As she made off, he got a small feel of her thighs. Baby was banging.

"Thank you King," she said, walking into the strip club.

A vibration went off in King's pocket. He checked his

Rolex and it was half past two. He pulled out his cell phone. The alarm went off. It was set to go off at 2:00 a.m. King's wife had set it to that time in feat that he'd fall asleep on the road.

Thinking of Maria, King called her cell number from his Verizon Wireless from the contacts list. She was worried sick by now, knowing Maria.

"Hello?" came Maria's voice, answering stealthily.

"Hey, it's me."

Maria whisked. Then fully into the phone, she said: "Honey, where you are you?"

"I'm on my way home Maria. I got in a little rode block on my way but should be there in a half hour."

"Okay King," Maria said.

King stumped the dirt off his shoes, then went into his cruiser and closed the door from the cold. "Honey everything alright?"

"Yes," she answered. "And if you're not home within 40 minutes, I am calling the police."

"I'll be home shortly. Bye."

They hung up. Wanting to check with his daughter Molly—age 10, King sent her number in afterward. Surprisingly, she picked up.

"Hey daddy! Is this a surprise?"

"Sort of, baby. Why did you ask that?"

"Because. You and mommy always play games when you're in the bedroom together."

Me and mommy? In the Bedroom? King thought maybe his kid had started school too late.

"I'm not in the bed with mommy. I'm on the road, Molly. Another long day's work on the streets. Keeping the bad guys away from the good guys. I'll be home soon.

That's all I wanted to tell you."

"Really?" Molly said. "Can you bring me something cool back, daddy? Like candy or a toy like you always do?"

"Always. Anything for my baby girl. Now I want you to get back to bed, hear. You got school tomorrow and need to get your rest."

"Hey daddy? If you're not home then who was that in the bedroom with mommy making all those noises?"

AMBITION

THE "R" IN ROGUISH

—

"I can't worry about no other man. You know why?" Lynn preached. "He ain't gone pay my bills and I ain't gone pay his." Lynn took a bite of his father's barbequed ribs.

Mrs. Motherhen, Lynn's mother, said, "Oh, stop that mad talk, boy."

Mr. and Mrs. Motherhen lived in a small house on a street off Old Winter Garden Road. Every month they tried to bring their kids together for a family event. Lynn, Lita, and Mack, the youngest three, were all married and lived in better houses than their parents did.

"I hear you Mr. Corrections Officer," hyped Mona. Mona was Arnold's contemporary girlfriend. "Yummy! This rib is delicious. What did you do to it?"

But he was long gone. About 40 minutes ago, Mr. Motherhen had shut the door to the master bedroom which was directly in front of the living room. He was rather dysfunctional in that way.

Mrs. Motherhen answered for him. "Marinated, then smoked them meat slow."

"Lynn you work tomorrow?" Arnold asked, flipping through channels to his parents HBO cable. Arnold was the oldest and the only one who did not own a home better than his parents did. In fact, he didn't have a house. He lived in a rented motel.

"You already know them scary crackers got me working. Crackers afraid to be in that jail overnight anyway."

"I heard that," Arnold chuckled. "But real talk, when you 'gonna get me a job? I mean we still blood ain't we?"

Even though his name was Arnold, the name "Low" had been attached to Arnold because of his reckless behavior and brush-in's with the law. As a youngster, he had run the streets, yet managed to graduate from high school. From there he entered the military and then quit after the traveling began to bore him; just dropped it like hot garbage.

Lynn didn't miss a bite of the baked beans on his plate. "It takes all my might to keep my job. Let alone get you a job," he said after a gulp of Hawaiian punch.

Lynn was the second oldest.

"Sure enough took you long enough to answer him," Lita peeped, the baby of the family. Lita lived in the best neighborhood, drove the nicest vehicle, and had the most expensive lifestyle. She had graduated from the University of Florida at 22 years old where she had met Bernard, her husband. She failed to tame him, and often worried herself sick about his promiscuity with other divas.

"Lynn," Arnold called. "Do the Correction Officer's still carry guns?"

"We got Tasers. They took guns out after an inmate shot an officer and escaped. Bastard's still on the run. I don't think he'll ever get caught."

Sitting on the couches across from "Low" was Lynn's wife. Dina was mute during these family get together's. One because she felt like she was the only outlaw there. And two because she'd been out of work since her and Lynn were married. She was guilty when Lynn would complain about his financial problems because she was in such an unproductive state herself. One good thing she was worth was having her mother watch their kids whenever she and Lynn wanted to be alone.

When she did speak, she usually asked a question. "Did Mack leave already Arnold?" she asked, eying Arnold, straight ahead.

"I guess," he replied. "Mama did Mack leave?"

Ms. Motherhen said, "Didn't you hear him when he said good bye? He left right after he made his plate."

"That's all he comes here for? To eat?" asked Lynn. "That boy needs to learn how to stay and talk to people. Shit!"

Ms. Motherhen always believed in defending her son. "You know that boy is so busy with his job and stuff that he doesn't have much time for nothing. You know how that is."

Lynn got up, threw his plate in the garbage, then made a large plate to go. "You about ready to leave Dina? Do we need to get the kids?"

"I guess," she said. "I'll have to call my mom again to see." Dina went to the door where Lynn was waiting. Arnold gave her a pat on the back as she passed.

"Goodbye Everybody. Bye Arnold." Dina exited the small house with a waving hand in the air. Lynn said his farewells and closed the door behind her.

"Bye. Nice to meet y'all," Mona beamed. Poor Mona. If Mona only knew: she'd never see them again.

Low gambled around with the remote control for a few moments. Out of all the channels his parents had on their HBO, he was not able to set his attention on one.

Before he got frustrated Low said, "Alright, I'm going

to be getting out of here too. It's about that business. Let's beat it Mona."

"Why you leaving so early?" asked Mona. "Lita is still here."

"I can do that," Lita said sharply.

"McLita Wynn Motherhen you be nice to Arnold's friend, hear?" Mrs. Motherhen pleaded.

"That's alright Mom," Mona said, rising in her heels. "Arnold's right. It *is* time for us to leave. So, I guess I'll see you next time. Tell Mr. Motherhen goodbye for me now. Chow."

Mona sidestepped Lita in the kitchen and outside into Arnold's put-put Toyota that they had stolen the night before.

"Alright Mom, I guess we're be leaving. I'll see you folks next time," Arnold said as he gave his mother a plump kiss on the cheek. He chucked up the deuce sign to Lita as he walked out of the house and said, "*Hastá la vista, Bebe*!"

"Good to see you again son. That reminds me of something: Where did you get that car out there?"

"Natural selection," he said. "Those least equipped with security will all be mine. Mysteriously mine mother."

"Be fair with Lynn, here. He still can't get over what happened with you and his ex-girlfriend. And I can't blame him either. He was fixing to marry that girl. And then you go and sleep with her behind his back. I can't blame Lynn."

Low the "Womanizer" had one thing to say before he left: "Another man's X is another man's treasure. Kidding ma. You know I'm my brother's keeper. I hope I am, at least."

—

Arnold loved to wear Polo. As he wore Polo pants, a Polo shirt, and Polo kicks, he floored the gas pedal of the raggedy Toyota. Mona rode shotgun.

"Arnold let me ride." Mona suggested.

"You don't have a license."

"Neither do you."

"Good point." Arnold admitted as he pulled into a parking lot in Save-Rite. He powered the car off and got out.

Mona wanted to know why they stopped. "Why we stop?"

"I want to get out and grab a few things. I still got some of the money that Dina gave me at my mom's. Stay put 'cause this won't take long."

Low slammed the driver's door shut but Mona got out of the car behind him anyway.

"What Dina giving you money for? You a Grown ass man."

Low politely took a deep breath. "Mind your fucking business. Get back in the car 'cause I told you this will only take a few," he said, turning his back and mumbling monotones as he went.

Meanwhile Mona maneuvered her model frame back into the car.

"Whoop Dee freaking do," she said to herself as she positioned herself into the driver's seat.

The keys had slid out Arnold's pocket without him noticing it!

"If it wasn't for me he'd have locked the keys inside

the car," Mona said. She started the vehicle up. "This is his only key because he got it from the bumper. Time to reward myself by a joy ride!"

And joy ride she did. She didn't get far though.

Approximately seven minutes went by until Arnold came out of the store and saw sprinkling red and blue cop lights beyond the road.

And then he noticed that his Toyota was missing. He flung the few grocery bags he had onto the bench and checked his right pocket. Sure enough, his keys were missing!

"Fuck!" he cursed himself as he ran toward the police scene up ahead.

When Low got there, ambulance trucks and a firefighter truck was posted around the put-put Toyota that was driven into a street light, being totally wrecked to the point of no return. If you thought it was wrecked before, you should see it now. The vehicle was now a piece of scrap metal.

"What happened?" Low asked an eyewitness standing by watching the firefighters search the vehicle.

"Dude some teenage girl totally wrecked this stolen car!" explained a tall adolescent. "Totally wicked! I saw her do it and she didn't even get hurt. The only reason she got caught was because a policeman was trailing her the whole time."

Low took a few steps back. "So she got caught, huh?"

"Caught as can be. Peep this, she wasn't even 18 yet."

Low stooped off the pavement and took a long stare at the scene.

"Kids these days," said one of the firemen. "How can you steal a car then wreck it? Right in front of a cop?"

"Shit happens," Low replied.

Low crossed the street from the self-inflicted accident. He would have to find another car and he would have to do it fast. He forgot about the groceries he had purchased earlier. He was angrier at himself for slipping like he had.

Arnold entered a CVS Store and shopped around looking for nothing in particular. He left wearing a pair of nerdy glasses, making him look his age, considering he is 32. He also purchases a lotto ticket before he left, stuffing it in his pocket. He walks for about a mile when he discovers a four floor parking lot that is laced with a lot of expensive cars by people with a lot of money.

Low goes probing. Passing Cadillac, Ford, Lincoln, Dodge. He stops and looks inside a GMC Suburban.

His shoes scuff the parking lot as he inspects the big SUV. Rain began to drizzle down from the sky outside the parking lot. Low felt a few drips land on his upper neck when he checked the rear bumper.

"Perfect," he said. Low found the magnetic key holder deep inside the body of the SUV just as the rain formed into a storm and started to pour down. Though the parking garage was blocked from outside weather, water came in anyway. Low swiftly opened the door like a ninja and confined him inside the safety of the baby semi-truck.

It was amazing to Low how many people hid spare keys under their bumpers, but yet many thieves insisted on the old fashioned way of breaking the locks. If he had known this in the past it would have saved him from plenty of trouble with the law.

Low woke the truck up in all the rain and started to back out. "Woof! Woof!" the engine revved. He decided to flip the radio on. The R&B station popped up and the reporter was in the middle of listing traffic problems in the area.

"...East Bound 1 has a hold up. A teenage girl has crashed a stolen car into a pole. Well, she survived and traffic is pretty slow. Also on Fort Street there is a traffic clog if you're heading north. All clear and smooth going south. And that's it for the traffic report. Over to you, Jay."

"Fuck!" Lawson thought as he rode out the garage. "What if my family sees Mona on the news?"

Arnold forgot to turn his windshield wipers on, so when he got outside he was caught in a frenzy trying to find the windshield wiper switch. The whole front window was blurred by rain, and Arnold was starting to panic. His vision was blurred. "C'mon!" he said as he hit button after button trying to turn the wipers on.

Not able to see anything before him, Arnold hit the brakes hard and brought the car to a Holt as a car horn came from beside him. He rolled his driver's window down, finding a car parked next to his and a gray haired white man furiously running toward him.

"Can't you see what's in front of you, you fucker!" he yelled. "If you hadn't stopped, you'd have run dead into that brick wall."

Up ahead was a one way outlet aligned by a large four foot concrete wall. There was no other exit or entrance.

"Sorry," Low said. "I couldn't find the windshield wiper switch. Understand I just got this car three days ago."

"Why isn't the paper tag on it then?" the man said. "Never mind. I work too hard for this. I shouldn't have to explain myself to some ignoramus who doesn't know how to drive."

The white man furiously stomped off with the adrenaline of a young lad and got into his car. And just after that, a police car came swerving up to them, blocking their exit paths. The policeman waited until the rain simmered down to get out, giving him time to run a scan through of their license plates.

He balked over to Low's car first and ordered him to get out and asked for his license. Low gave it to him. Next, the policeman went to the gray haired man and ordered the same thing. After looking over his license and hearing his complaint, he let the old guy drive off in his Lincoln Town car.

"Why he get to go?" Low asked as the cop came toward him.

The cop ignored his question. "How long ago did you take this picture?"

"A while back," Arnold said.

"It resembles you, Mr. Maynard. For the most, it looks like somebody else. When is your birthday?"

Arnold remembered this. "December 29th, 1982."

"Are you an organ donor?"

"Um, yes," Low guessed, tensing up. "If I can remember."

"*If you can remember*," the cop mocked. "What is your address?"

"Jersey Shore, New Jersey. Then its 4040..."

The cop made a strong move and bodied slammed Low against the GMC. "Wrong!" he said, slapping handcuffs onto Lows fighting wrists.

"When I was scanning your license plate I noticed

that this truck belonged to a black woman so I thought maybe were her relative. But now I know you're not because your last name is different plus this isn't even your real license, if yours at all."

"Off to the pound we go," said the officer as he threw Arnold into the back of his cop car. Off to the pound they went.

Thirty-third precincts was not a jail you wanted to be in. The people in it were roguish and the Corrections Officers were brutal. Two big heavy guard's ushered Low into a cell where at least a dozen men were waiting in. This was Low's fourth stop at this precinct.

"Is Lynn here?" Arnold asked a guard walking by. "When can I use the phone?"

Low and behold, this was also the jail in which Arnold's brother, Lynn, worked at.

A whole day went by until Lynn found his brother in the precinct area of the jail. "Arnold!" Lynn called out, opening the lock to greet his brother. Lynn was bigger and healthy. The other prisoners in the cell knew not to jump stupid.

"You in trouble again huh? Do you have a lawyer yet?" Lynn scolded, disappointed in his brother.

Low sighed. "They say their getting one for me. Fall back."

"Fall back? Didn't the judge tell you the next time you go to jail you may face up to 10 years in prison? You're not a kid anymore more. It's time for you to act like it. Mentioning kids, Dina told me she saw that girlfriend of yours on the news. Cop caught her after she totally wrecked a stolen car. She was only 17, Arnold."

"Yea. Too bad. But I try Lynn. What you think I land

in here on purpose? Everyone isn't blessed with a good job like you got."

Lynn grabbed Arnold by the arm and made it look like he had him under control as a fellow Correction Officer passed.

"How long they say you going to be here?" Lynn asked.

"Probably a week like last time. Actually that was something I was hoping you could help me with. If I make bail I can get out and they can only try me as an ordinary without looking at my criminal history."

"I don't know about this Arnold. How much is bail?"

"$15,000. Nothing more."

"That's a lot of money for me. I got children to feed," Lynn said painfully.

"I know. If you do me this favor, I would pay you back twice the number within a year tops. Guaranteed."

"I don't know. I'll think about this. You need to use the jail phone?"

"Yea, as a matter of fact I do," Arnold said. "Thanks for reminding me."

"Go down into this room and into that next one. There shouldn't be much of a line. When you're done hold your hand up and one of the officers will take you back to your cell. I'm gone."

Lynn went back to work and Low went into the phone room. Like Lynn said, there was no line for the phones so Low punched a number in quickly as possible. "Dina is this you?"

"Hello," the housewife picked up. "Who is this?"

"It's me. Arnold," he said. "Hey I just talked to your husband in jail."

"Holy...Arnold don't tell me you're in jail again?"

"Please believe it."

"Well, what do you know? Why is it so hard for you and black men in general, to stay out of trouble?"

The guard on duty called out from behind Low: "You have one minute left!"

"Look Dina I don't have much time left on the phone. The judge may have me in for three strikes this time if I'm convicted. But if I make bail they won't be able to touch me. I talked to your husband today and he said he'll think about it. Can you do a little convincing for me?"

"Wow," she said. "I'll try and do what I can. Say, how much is bail?

"Bail is 15 thousand. I appreciate you for everything."

"Damn that's a lot of money. You're not a kid no more. Lynn ass is always complaining about paying bills these days. But as crazy as this sound: Count me in."

"Thanks. By Dina."

The phone went dead. "TIMES UP!" shouted the guard from above.

A bulky guard grabbed Low by the collar and basically launched him back into his jail cell. "Sleep light. Don't let the bed bugs bite."

Low didn't see Lynn again until the next afternoon. When he approached his cell, Lynn's body language screamed a message so vulgar even his co-workers didn't say anything to him.

"Hey, what's up? How's everything moving?" Low greeted his brother. "What's wrong with you? You look tired."

Lynn curled his mouth up, making an expression that said, "Shut your face and don't speak!"

"I've got the money," Lynn said meaningfully. "I took ten thousand out my account and I took out a 5 thousand dollar loan that Dina is supposed to pick up today. She will be coming here to bail you out. If you don't mind."

Low was overcome with the spirit of mastermind. He felt like a genius!

"Really? Lynn I...I...don't know what to say."

"Then don't. Dina should be here within a few hours so just hold tight. I'll be back to escort you out when they call your name to go."

Low didn't have a cellmate, so he just walked back and forth in the charcoal cell gripping the iron bars impatiently until he heard familiar footsteps again. "Lynn. That you?"

"No, it's Dina."

Low dashed to the front of the cell and saw Dina with a card in her hand and a big duffel bag that was full of something important enough to be strapped to her body.

"Dina! What the Hell are you doing here?"

The card Dina held in her hand she swiped it though and the cell slowly slid open. "Ready to make bail?" Dina asked. "I'm breaking you out. I got all the cash we need in my bag."

"How did you get through here?" asked Low, being yanked out the cell by a frantic hand from Dina.

Dina led Low through the halls, trying to calm him down.

"You should be happy I'm breaking you out of this place after what you told me. But if you really want to know, I copied Lynn Jail ID yesterday. When I came here to request bail, I escaped as they were about to take the money. If we can make it out, then we have the world.

Just me and you Arnold."

"I didn't know you were going to do this Dina! You have a family!" If there was a mirror nearby, a scary cat is what Low would see in the reflection. "And even if we do get away—"

A screech came loudly from around the corner and Dina was face to face with her husband, Lynn. Low was beside her. Surprise Bitches!

"Dina?" Lynn asked. Lynn was shock like a deer in headlights. "Arnold!" Holy Shit! "How in the *World* did you get in here Dina? I hope this isn't what it looks like!" he barked, burning at Dina.

Dina was frozen. She looked over at Low. That was all she could do. And Low made a move.

Low jumped on Lynn so quick that Lynn never saw it coming. Low moved like the invisible 13th ghost that could not accept its fate. Low punched Lynn twice in the face and choked his neck. Lynn struggled but he was still a trained C.O. Lynn absorbed the hits by the rageful inmate then gained power and rolled up on top of Low and started punching him, beating him back to sanity.

Dina stood there in a state of hallucination. Quickly, she spotted the big Taser gun hanging from Lynn's uniform pocket. She made a run towards the nasty brawl, snatching the Taser gun from his possession.

Lynn spun around, finding his wife clutching his 12 watt Taser gun. "And what do you think you're doing?" he asked.

Dina aimed the Taser at her once beloved husband and said, "I'm done with doing everything your way. After today, you figure out how to do it all by yourself."

She pressed the gun and let Lynn have a dose of radiation. Now, he lay on the ground, unconscious and twitching.

"Darn girl! That was hell of a shock," Low said. "We got to get out of here."

"I know. Grab him and we'll carry him back to your cell. Then we'll have to cover as much ground as possible."

Low grabbed his brother and Dina helped push "the" unconscious man back into the jail cell then locked it shut. Albeit the noise they had made, no one seemed to notice. Before they shut the cell door, Arnold snatched the Correction's Officer Shirt off Lynn and buttoned it onto himself.

"This will have to do," Lynn said as he and Dina went to try and escape from the jail.

All of a sudden, Lynn's voices came from the cell, real weakly and crumble like. "You won't make it out," he said.

Low pretended like he didn't hear him at first, but then turned around to face his own brother. "What did you say?"

"You heard me," he said. "C'mon, Arnold. Is this really worth it? I think she has the money in her bag. It's only roughly what, fifteen grand? How long can you live off that before you get caught, Arnold?"

"I won't get caught Lynn. It's already too late to stay anyway. I bet the cameras have already caught us. Matter fact, I bet them people coming now."

As Low said this, he scurried off with Dina throughout the jail cells.

"After all I've done for you, you going to do me like this? Again? Brother? With my woman. Again?" Lynn yelled, twitching out of consciousness. The Taser's side effects were serious. "That's just wrong." Then he fell completely out of consciousness, falling to sleep.

"I didn't know she was coming," Lynn yelled back, fleeing his hardest as the jail alarm siren rung loud and the place began to lock itself up.

"*Intruder Alert! Intruder Alert!*" The alarm repeated this.

"No matter what, we are still blood," Low moped, getting emotional, and scurrying in Dina's clutch. "I failed to be my brother's keeper but I will always love you Lynn. I love you."

SPEAKING OF MONEY

—

People like me fall into bad habits. The worst part about it is we never realize it until it's too late. Until that final bell rings to end the day and we end up wishing we would have caught ourselves before it was over. Bad as a habit it may be, I personally never acknowledge it until it costs me money. After checking out a library book, I search my pockets for cash to get some gas with and as I reach my car parked on the side of the street, I fling my paraphernalia into the passenger seat of my car. As I am about to crank the car up, I notice a rectangular white card on the outside of my window that reads UNPAID PARKING METER. I read the rest backwards: **TEKCIT GNIKRAP 003$.** I hammer the steering wheel with both fists and the horn blows a raggedy tune, "Huungk!"

I went in the County Library for a few minutes and, joy, I get handed another parking ticket. Speaking of money.

Yesterday, if I can remember, I parked in the handicapped space at Baby's R US for a good 3 hours and when we came out, Fellisha and I found my car victim to bird droppings. My car is old but I keep it clean and shiny.

Still, my fiance and I got into the Thunderbird and drove on home. On the way, I rubbed her 6 month belly and whispered, "Only the best for my little man...I am going to buy you a golden spoon once I get right with my company. Hold me to that, Champ."

I am a soon to be father and I am elated beyond pride.

Accelerating onto traffic, I turn my windshield wipers on and let the ticket flutter off in my rear view mirror. At least now I would have an excuse why I didn't pay it.

Our apartment complex ventured out a quarter gallon of gas from where I worked and a bespectacled 6 miles changed on the 1989 odometer from the library.

One of many analyst for the Television Network, I checked out a book titled *Natures Behavior,* to get background information for the book that I am seeking to publish: My debut nonfiction project that I worked on for some years now.

The first Hess gas station is on the right side of the road so I crept the Thunderbird under pump eight, braking as I line my gas can with the pump. I head in and out the store with $10 worth to pump. While refueling, I pulled out my old and outdated chirp phone and called David B, my literary agent. He works for me free.

"Hello?" the agent answered.

"David it's me, James. I've finally come up with a title for my book: *Broke by Tomorrow.* How's that sound?"

The sub heading will be: Effective Ways to Save Money, the S in *Save* will be a dollar sign. But I decide not to tell him this. David's imagination is not very perceivable.

"Not bad," David said, "but it still may not stand well with the publishers we're going for."

"How's it looking with Grand Central?"

"They're still neutral but it's not looking good."

A light pause occurred and I hear David voice again as the gas guzzle pinches to a stop. "They have had your piece for over a week and a decision should have been made by now."

Music to my ears. Where had I heard this hit song before? I finished my nonfiction book with high hopes that it would be published to a greedy audience and sell big. This wasn't good. "Dave, come on. Tell me it's not the ignoring treatment again."

Grand Central was not the first Publisher to deny me or delay a decision on a publishing deal. After I completed my manuscript, Dave and I sent the material to various publishers for the same result. Eventually, something had to give.

"That's what it appears Mr. Diapers," Dave said. "The manuscript may not be good enough, maybe long enough either. All I can tell you is that we have our backs against the walls. No responses. The book may have been a bad idea from the start."

"Thanks for the update," I said. No more talk was needed.

I shuffle the cell phone back in my pocket and start the car. All ten dollars' worth.

Reversing out the gas station, I merge back with traffic and take the fast lane to Wood-ridge Apartments. While driving I see a billboard ad that reads, "*Stop Killing, Start Dreaming.*" Of all things. I can't help thinking of my current situation. The ad is relevant. To live a certain life people have to trade in their aspirations and dreams.

When I arrive at my destination, I find a spot among the packed cars next to a handicap spot. I don't see Felli-sha's Honda. There is no tow truck in sight so unless a premature water break occurred, she better have a damn good excuse why she is not home at nearly 8 o'clock in the day.

Unfortunately there is.

I fumble the key around in the lock, not able to see clearly under the buildings shadow. Suddenly I hear the knob jingling from someone's movements and the door flings open. Fellisha, god bless her heart, is standing in front of me, pregnant belly and all.

One of my hands is full, but the other is free so I rub it against my soon-to-be child. "Fellisha where's your car?" I ask.

"I sold it."

"You did what!" I spit out, even though I heard her the first time.

Fellisha pushes my hand away from her, away from *us,* and starts walking toward the kitchen. "James, come on. We can barely afford to buy baby food, let alone another working vehicle. I've been trying to sell that car for a while now. I finally got what I wanted for it: Five Hundred. It didn't work anyway. You knew that."

I shrug. "Pumpkin, you know I'm about to get that hot shot promotion at my job. Then you'll be able to drive whatever you want. And when I get a deal on my book, we'll move to a nicer place in the suburbs."

Fellisha leaves for the kitchen. I hear dishes clattering in the sink. "James our wedding is in seven months after I give birth to Miracle."

The pain in her voice could not be hidden. "This time I'm not pushing the wedding back for anything. Either we get married or we don't."

Miracle? Since when had she come up with a name

for my child? "So you came up with a name for our baby? What else have you done that I don't know of?"

The dish washing stopped. Fellisha's voice rang out loud and clear. "Miracle it is. Since you don't have any say these days. What if your plans don't work out? Huh? We'll be stuck like this for the rest of our lives. Won't we? It will take a *miracle* to raise a child in these environments. And when are you going to buy some dish detergent?"

I think back to that ad I saw earlier and compare it to what Fellisha had just said.

Stop Killing, Start Dreaming.

For the next week or two, Fellisha goes through the days talking on the phone, hardly speaking. Rarely do I see her eat. I hear her talking to her friends, and most threatening, her parents.

I over hear one of her conversations while doing my weekly laundry: "… I know dad. But now I'm starting to have second questions…How was church today?"

Fellisha and her family is Catholic. I wasn't raised in any specific religion but if someone asked me I'd just say, "Christian."

Fellisha and I have never missed a day of Sunday Church. However, her attitude leads her to breaking our tradition. This is very bad. She would substitute Jesus to be on the telephone?

This was bad.

I didn't like it. This wasn't her. I tried coaxing her to attend church, but she'd just put an index finger to her mouth or hold up the phone to show how busy she was.

On another note, I would prefer Mr. Haynes on the phone with my fiance over the stricter Mrs. Haynes.

A while back, Mr. Haynes and I had gone to church

together. It was just the two of us and I found Mr. Haynes to be quite the believer. He'd rise and clap and rejoice. About half way through service, the pastor called for anyone and everyone with financial problems to stand up.

"I'd like to ask for anyone whose to be a cheerful giver to come up to the alter.

Mr. Haynes gave me a shove of approval with his left elbow.

"You should go up there, Hot Shot," he said, giving me another elbow to eat.

At that time, work was steady and Fellisha and I were maintaining well. I knew the secular Mr. Haynes thought highly about their daughter's boyfriend. Plus it wasn't no telling what Fellisha had blown their Old Italian heads up with.

Seeing only a handful of people standing, I rose from my feet and stepped forward, relieving myself from Mr. Haynes consistent elbow.

"Any man able to serve God's children, I challenge you to step up today," the pastor said.

"I have money," I said out loud. I walked on stage.

I remember looking down from the stage and counting a total of six people standing. Six people in need of financial help. Cool, I remember thinking to myself. I could do this; I had 7 twenty dollar bills in my pocket.

"May Lord bless you young man whose name shall be written in Heaven's gate," said the priest.

This was a church Mr. Haynes wanted me to see because of ministry. Fellisha and her mother didn't come and I couldn't blame them. The priest had hypnotic powers. Attending a friend's baby shower was Fellisha and her mom's excuse.

I could see a bunch of church people dozed off in church. Then someone from behind me shouted: "Sir, come down here so we can discuss the money you're going to give away."

So there I went from the platform down to the offices below.

When I entered a room in the back, safe from view of the church audience, a man who I summed up to be the pastor shook my hand. "Hello how are you doing, sir. I am delighted you have volunteered to take part in this give away at our church."

He offered me a seat. I refused.

Then he motioned with his hand and suddenly a short man whom I never ever seen before came forth. He extended his small hand. "How are you doing this fine morning sir," he said. "We have six needy Christians out there in need of financial assistance. We like to pinch in and help some of our members every so often in any way we can. As a decor of the fundraiser community, I am pleased that such a fine gentleman as yourself has stepped forward to offer to those less fortunate. We truly are blessed to have you here with us today. All I need is your name. Sit so we can get started."

How much money was I supposed to give away? They hadn't mentioned a number. Yet.

"I'm Mr. Diapers."

"Great. I'll get things going immediately," he said and walked out the room, leaving the rest of us there.

Suddenly I heard his voice boom from the microphone on the speaker system. "Good evening ladies and gentlemen. I'd like for all of the folks standing to remain so. The appointed man agreeing to give away his money is

Mr. Diapers. He will be coming onto the stage shortly. But first I would like everyone to know that he will be giving away $1000 to each of the six members standing."

At this, applause thundered throughout the church. "Yay'!"

One Thousand Dollars! They wanted me, poor little James Diapers, to give $1,000 to 6 different people? That would've been 6 thousand grand. I had about one hundred and forty dollars on me. And that's the truth. At the time, I only had 800 bucks in my savings account!

Lord have mercy!

I politely left the room and found an exit door to the back of the church. As I tripped from going so fast, I heard the pastor say, "And here he is—Mr. Diapers here to deliver some spiritual words before he gives his money away. Give a much needed round of applause for Mr. Diapers!"

Out of the back of the building, I jolted for it like I was in my old track team days. There was no way I could give away 6 grand. To this day, Mr. Haynes along with the rest of Meola Mist Church cannot solve the enigma of the vanishing Mr. Diapers.

That was what happened when you did speak of money.

Now I am on the precipice of success and at the same time the brink of failure. The following day is a Monday. I wake up in the morning and head to Visual Telecommunications in my old Thunderbird.

After finding a spot to park in the Employee parking lot, I make for the revolving door entrance with my equipment bag in hand. As I approach my place of work, I feel a new energy surfacing from its vicinity. Something has changed. I can feel it.

I brim the door open and almost collide with Mr. Timsdale, my communications manager. At 7 in the morning he is hard to see because of his dark skin and all. Hell, he's pitch black.

"James!" he yells excitedly. "How are you this morning? Today is a very special day for you it is. I don't want to spoil your surprise but you'll be delighted by the news lying in your office. The paper is in your mail box. Congratulations James!"

We shake hands and I watch "Midnight" leave. I turn around, going as I fast as I could to get to my mail box trying not to look rushed, thinking that Mr. Timsdale could only be talking about one thing.

I open the envelope and read it. *'Congratulations James Diapers! On behalf of Visual TV we will be promoting you to the position of TV Director.'*

A promotion indeed! *Joy*! I could hear the heavens rejoicing! I place the card back and unload my bag in dazzle.

"Whoo!" I leave for the studio holding my camera in one hand. I was now the lead person over the entire television crew. Miracles do happen! My paycheck would be nearly doubled, not even mentioning my holiday bonuses. I couldn't wait to tell Fellisha!

Right now, though, I had a piece to shoot. Our writing crew recently got a television job to work on from ABC news and they were finished with the writing. Work was work, and it was time for me and the Dream Team to produce.

I would have to put off telling Fellisha until later.

Actually, I ended up misjudging it. While filming, I could only think about money, and the time began to fly.

Money was on my mind. My family, my future. Everything. My Miracle, on the way. The directors and produc-
ers kept hitting me with different critiques and before we
knew it, lunch hour was upon us.

"Hey Boss, what you going to do with that extra thir-
ty minutes," shot one of the script writers.

"That's Right!" I yell in complete jubilation. He was
right! Now that I was the new TV Director I would have a
full hour lunch. My benefits were looking beautiful!

I lay the camera on the floor on top of a pile of trash.
I grab my car keys then head out the door.

Instead of calling Fellisha, I will do the real thing and
tell her in person!

Or should I say in pregnancy?

A worker was stenciling the *A* of *DIAPERS* outside
of my new director's door. The company would have to
remodel the area. Back in the car, I foot the gas petal
driving along the highway. Soon my chirp phone rings.

"Hello? James is you there?"

It's David B. Jesus Christ… I did not want to speak
to him. But I answered nonetheless.

"Yes. What's up?" Why the hell are you calling me at
this hour?

"Two words," he said. "Grand Deal. Grand Central
has decided to give you a deal on their terms. If you agree,
your book will be published within nine months and you
will receive a handsome advance."

The phone fumbled in my hand as I clasped it as a
traffic light changed. "David… don't BS me. What kind of
advance are we talking here?"

"We're talking 6,000 dollar ball park range to a new
author with no writing background whatsoever."

I couldn't believe my ears. I'm sure David was just as surprised as I was that Grand Central, a major publisher, was offering such a large amount of money to an unproven writer! "David...by all means—this—This is unbelievable! They're offering 6 grand up front. All I'll have to do is pay you and the rests mine!"

David's voice changed. "Exactly. I'll get my ten percent. If the deal stands, you can keep the $5,400. James they want to talk to us both over the phone tomorrow morning. During the conversion, you let me do the talking. I'll give you some more details in the morning. Take care, James."

I shove the phone in my pocket as I park my car in the apartment parking lot. I could not believe the events that had taken place. First, I had been promoted by my company, which I had been anticipating for a while now. And now this: I was finally about to get a blockbuster deal on my book that I had written all by myself...Wicked!

It felt too grand to be true. I would have to be careful how I told Fellisha. I mean she might enter into premature birth!

As I candidly rip the door open, a yellow piece of construction paper immediately strikes my attention because I never remember it being there.

"Fellisha?" I called out.

No answer.

"Fellisha, you here boo? I got some news to tell you."

I go to where the yellow paper is on the floor.

"Tell me how our little Miracle is doing. Fellisha..."

Nothing again. Either my fiancé' is deaf or she is not in the apartment.

Then I pick the paper up and notice the familiar

looking handwriting. It reads:

"Goodbye James, I'm sorry it had to end like this. By the time you read this, the abortion will already be over. I can go on no further living under these conditions. As for me, I'll be settling somewhere new, a location you should never know. The wedding is off, and James, we're done. The wedding ring is on the kitchen sink where the detergent should be. Use the ring to buy yourself some detergent— you'll need it. It's not that I don't love you it's just that I can't take it anymore. I cannot live like this. Take care.

Fellisha, Love, Always.

An abortion. Miracle? My Miracle. Now all gone along with Fellisha? The whole thing felt sickening, so out of place, like I was nothing. I drop the paper and place my hands over my eyes and begin to sink into my clothes. Tears start to make their way onto the crevices of my eyelids.

"Stop Killing, Start Dreaming…"

And then suddenly a thought hits me like a ton of light bulbs. The note read, *"By the time you read this, the abortion will be over—…"*

She had thought I would be reading this letter 4 hours to the time. She didn't think I would come home on my lunch break. There was a good chance that I could catch her before she went through with the abortion. I could still catch her and tell her all the great news! She'd be overjoyed. Surely, she'd come home then.

I dart to the kitchen, knocking ornaments down as I enter. I spot the ring and grab it, blowing a giant cockroach to Kingdom Come on the counter. I rush out the door and back into the Thunderbird. This time I would do it the right way. We would get married on the spot! To hell with what everyone thought.

I pull out of the driveway and foot it as hard as I can to Shan's Hospital. My first child was about to be killed by my fiancé' all because she was sick of being in a relationship with me. All because I had failed to provide for my family.

And now I am on the race of my life. This is what happens when you didn't speak of money.

I DON'T BLAME ME

—

U nder any other circumstances, the situation may have seemed funny.

The ten-year old G5 Bullet engine Jet, descended at an arresting rate in the afternoon sun. A male control pilot and a comparably young lady dressed in safety gear sat next to each other in the pilot seats, glancing cock-eyed at the sky as white clouds settled in. The pilot is on the controls with every imaginable flying precaution strapped to his person. The younger woman takes in the lifetime view as a skinny runway angles up below the jet within a dozen mile radius. Handy, beneath her lap, lays a folder full of legal documents.

At this moment, the statement orbits in the air between them:

"Listen. I've never landed a plane before."

Eavlyn turned to stare at this man sitting in the pilot's seat. The guy was perspiring. His captain crunch overcoat was soaking and his collar was damp. His complexion was changing into a sour purple color, his broad shoulders crouching up.

"What do you mean you never landed?" Eavlyn demanded. Coming from Virginia, an hour had passed since she had stepped onto this flight.

"I flew in Vietnam and stuff. But whenever I got near landing, the flying instructor took over because I had bad

posture," he revealed. "I watched and followed her proce-
dure so I could learn. But I actually never landed on my
own."

"You've better be freaking me!"

The man shut his eyes for a few seconds. This was
not good. A few minutes earlier, the sky had gone from
low forecast to cloudy. Eavlyn could still make out the ma-
trix of buildings underneath them. The SunTrust skyline
was eminent in addition to the top of the Wachovia Bank
building on which they were landing.

"Don't panic..." the pilot mumbled. "I can get us
down. I still know what I'm doing. But I might need a little help to land us properly. I need you to see if there is a
switch at the bottom of the pilot's initiation launch control..."

Eavlyn was uneasy.

"Me?" She should never got onto this plane with this
man. When, and if, they landed, she'd tell her god-son she
needed re-compensation. And she wasn't thinking a verbal
apology.

"Yes, you. I just need you to pull the switch while I
levitate us down on the red X."

Eavlyn erupted. "I don't know anything about flying—"

"I just need you to pull the switch," the pilot ordered.
"I need you to levitate the jet so we can then lower it
down on the X. It's the top of a building so the runway is
steep."

"Why would you fly a plane if you don't know how to
land it?"

Eavlyn shut her eyes to keep her panic level from rising. She was going to die at the hands of an idiot. She

should have stayed in Virginia. Why did she let her god-son talk her out of leaving her natural environment?

"It's not a life or death ordeal here," the older man gasped. "Either you pull the switch and we land slow and graceful or you don't and we land awkwardly, damaging the jet."

Reluctant, Eavlyn acceded. "Tell me when," she said as the Bank building swallowed up the view of the G5 jet's and tiny people could be seen down below. The air began to clear and the old man went to work. Hitting switches and buttons, Eavlyn thought the pilot spoke a different language into the intercom as he controlled the Jet above the targeted X like a magician. He was speaking English, but Eavlyn couldn't understand the terminology.

"Okay, see that switch lying between us?" he gasped. "When I say, 'Hit it', you flip it to the other side and that should settle us down nice and smooth."

Down below, Eavlyn could see people milling around the Big X where they were to land. Eavlyn couldn't make out any face in particular, but, when she got down, and if she got down, she'd give her god-son a piece of her mind.

Minutes went by until the old man leveled the plane just above the X. The pedestrians below were a blur. Eavlyn felt ashamed that the jet might crash terribly below them and the pedestrians would be left totally unaware of their fate.

The pilot woke her up. "You ready? Hold on!"

He paces it. The jet levitated down with a vibration. "Hold on tight. Down we go!"

Pacing steady, he said "Almost!" They could feel the charge of the uncontrolled jet.

"Hit it!"

Eavlyn hit the plug as the G5 engine drained energy and gained control.

"You did it!" the pilot yelled.

Instinct took over. "Just get us down. I swear I am never flying again!" spurted Eavlyn.

The jet slowly shimmied down onto the X like a caterpillar sliding down a fruit tree. The pilot worked like a music producer, pressing buttons until the jet landed completely, after what had seemed like a funeral service.

Moving at an unprecedented speed, Eavlyn unstrapped herself and cracked open the passenger seat. She moved so fast that her folder dropped on the ground of the G5 as she got out.

The sweating pilot said, "You dropped your folder."

"Thanks," she said truly fallacious. *Great*, Eavlyn thought. *Now I almost lose the very thing that I need.*

Eavlyn had brought the stack of papers exactly as her god-son requested her to do. Her God son needed a favor and she was the only soul who could help him. As far as why he needed the favor, she still needed some details on that. But that is what she would get here at the bank. After her god-son's mom had died, Eavlyn was now the closest thing to a friend he had. Also, she had promised his mother to always be there for him. And Eavlyn couldn't break a promise.

No matter how much Eavlyn didn't agree with the situation, no matter how much she didn't believe in this, she couldn't break a promise. Now could she?

She gathered herself. The faces that were once blurs were now close with personal features.

From the front of the jet came a familiar looking middle-aged man. "Eavlyn. It is I," he said in a forceful

Russian tongue.

"Hanley!" Eavlyn naturally embraces her god-son.

They tightly coil each other, hugging. Tightly. It wasn't every day they saw each other. When the embrace was over, Eavlyn looked over her long lost god-son. Hanley had the rough features of someone forty years old despite his latent youth.

Hanley had traveled across many continents, visiting gambling spots, and trouble was mixed in wherever he went. Hanley made a living out of dodging death and ill will. Under excruciating pressure, he had gambled in a top-notch casino in Europe against the Russian Mob. And he had won nearly one million dollars. After he got the money, he stealthily fled from the back door of the casino. The Mob was not far off his trail.

Hanley was savvy with his escape though. He made slick turns, rude skips, and meaner hops. He was soon on an express train steaming to London. He had lost the Mob!

From there, Hanley laid low. He refused to check into any hotels or to used his debit card for any transactions. He knew that the Mob was lurking. He bombed around until he found a flight going to America.

After countless endeavors of "hitting the big lick," Hanley was destined to attain this jackpot.

Once in America, he called Eavlyn, his closest thing to a friend, and told her to bring all her legal documents and bank accounts with her on the private flight he had scheduled for her at the Virginia airport. He told her the plane would be flying to a Wachovia in New York City. Wachovia was his bank.

Surveying his god-mother, he was unhappy with what

he saw. "Why were you looking so spoiled when you got out of the jet?"

"I'll tell you in private," Eavlyn said. Together they went toward the stair rail on the top of the building. A Wachovia associate greeted them as they stepped down the steps.

"Hi," the elated banker said. "Are you Eavlyn? I've been told so much about you."

She extended her hand to Eavlyn. Eavlyn looked at her hand as if it was a piece of crap. Merile, the banker, caught on and said, "Nice to meet you." Then she turned around to lead them to her office. Eavlyn was not in the mood.

"Hanley? You never told me why you brought me here."

Hanley hadn't intended to. Not yet. It was too early. The Mob was still chasing: the mob never forgot. That was the motto. One million dollars was a lot of money. The reality was that he would now be on the run for the rest of his life because of that. He understood this and wanted to get no one involved. He was planning to wire three quarters of the million into one of Eavlyn's accounts. This would be for family, Eavlyn included. The rest of the money he'd keep, gamble with, and live off. Hanley had done the math. He could live the rest of his life on $250,000 K.

"I will tell you," he insisted. "But alone."

"What's with you and that fake accent?"

Leading her clientele down to the extravagant guest services, Merile offered them refreshments in the cafe. A soft classical song was playing in the bank.

"Oh, yes," Eavlyn said, shortchanging the cup of tea

and entree' she had received from Merile.

Hanley declined the water. He stood like a kid in a candy store, gazing around the bank. Out of the exclusive gambling casino's he had been inside of, the state of art design of this Wachovia was top notch. Never had he been in a bank like this before. Only in New York.

"How many floors does this bank have?" he asked.

"Too many," Merile said. People ask her this a lot.

Merile took control of her clients. "Whenever you guys are ready, I'll be waiting in my office," she said, pointing to where her office was. "You remember where it was Mr. Fotron?"

"Yes, Merile. We'll be there in a second."

Glad that Merile's loquacious endeavors had ended, Eavlyn forgot why she was there for a moment.

Hanley made his move. Pulling Eavlyn to the side, he stated:

"Eavlyn, there is something I need to tell you. Recently at a gambling casino in Russia I came up big— winning one million dollars. Unfortunately, the Mob was there. Now they are after me. That's where you come in. Eavlyn you are the closest person I know. I can give you three quarters of the million by wiring it to your account. I want you to sort it out between my kids, my mother's grave, my father, and yourself. I'll take the rest and flee."

Eavlyn wondered. "Why don't you just the call the police, rocket scientist?"

"I can't," Hanley testified. "This involves money, Eavlyn. American police are scared of the Russian Mob. They'd send me to the Feds. The Feds would try and protect me, just like a witness protection program. I'd be dead in a week."

"What does M.O.B. stand for?"

"Money over bullshit. And if you don't bulk up, I'd think you weren't taking me serious." Hanley glanced over at Merile's office. "Don't you want the money?"

"Yeah," Eavlyn said. "But I also want my life. If these Mob people are after you, then what makes you think they won't hunt *me* down?"

She was unsettled. Now she regretted taking the flight to the Big Apple. She yanked her folder up, stuffing it inside her purse.

"Eavlyn I need you." he begged. "You promised my mother you'd always be there for me!"

Hanley's mother died on New Year's Day. A stroke hit her in the morning during a heinous migraine. After being rushed to the hospital, her heartbeat could not be stabilized. She was dead by noon at age 48.

"I did," she confirmed. "But how can I be there for you if I can't even take care of myself?"

Nothing was left of Hanley's Russian accent. "Betrayer! You're betraying your best friend's one wish! Why don't you just sleep on it?"

By now, Merile had stepped out of her office for a peek at the action.

"Fine," Eavlyn said as she skimmed across the marble floor. Once she was inside the elevator, she said: "I'll sleep on it!"

Sleep on it she did. She registered at the Hilton's a few blocks away from Wachovia. She got a massage from some hunk and moistened herself in the hot tub. Room service she ate. And then slept on it for almost sixteen hours straight.

By any means, was Eavlyn rich. She had not even

planned to stay one day in New York but sometimes, life was unpredictable. This was the moral of the story. If anything, her fifty plus years of living in this cold world had taught her something. Controlling other people, things, or places was impossible. The only thing that she could count on was herself. Her husband had fretted away from her. He was there one day and then she woke up one day and he was gone. Her kids had forsaken her too. She had been abandoned by her family. So all she had now was herself.

Which wasn't much...or was it? Eavlyn was on the verge of having her boon-dock fort in Virginia paid for. She had a Grand Marquis paid off, all hers, with cash. And she had a garden big enough to be a vegetation producer for the state.

Now here she was, sleeping in the city that never did. Although New York was the "city that never sleeps," it was the place where dreams were alive and hearts fueled by them. Just about all the people she saw walking by were doing so with an extraordinary force pushing them. This was the adrenaline to control the things that they could, to feed their family before they fed themselves.

Eavlyn checked out the Hilton an hour ago. She had done some sporadic splurging while walking the strip. She had bought some lingerie, just for a souvenir, and a few more items since she was certain she would never come to New York again. A homeless man stopped to sell her an exquisite dress and she would have bought it except she feared it was stolen.

As she opened the door to the same Wachovia Bank, Eavlyn looked to see if Hanley or Merile were around. She did not see them.

Eavlyn went inside and stepped to the desk clerk. But

a banker was in pursuit and happened to suddenly brush by her.

"Excuse me?" she asked. "Is Merile here today?"

"Aw, yes," the banker identified. "Do you want me to retrieve her for you?"

"No." Eavlyn said, pulling the envelope from her purse. "Can you tell her this is from one of her clients?" Eavlyn handed it over to the banker.

"Sure. Is there anything else I can help you with?"

"No thank you," Eavlyn said, already walking out of the bank.

Instead of risking her livelihood in person, the disloyal god mother chose to drop off a sealed letter stating to Hanley that she could not help him. Why? How come? Her life was more valuable than any amount of U.S. currency. It had taken her to come to New York to understand this.

As far as Hanley was concerned, he would have to figure it out for himself. He had gotten himself into an incredible dilemma and would have to get himself out of it. This was not Eavlyn's battle. She knew how rough he had had it growing up. His best friend died in the 1st grade in a fire. He had witnessed the only uncle he knew drown and then be eaten by great white sharks. The only woman he loved, his mother, passed away when he was 20 years old. After that, his mother's death scarred him. He had pledged celibacy when he was 18, but ended up forfeiting all of his dignity after her death, turning himself out.

Eavlyn knew the story.

Another thing implanted in her brain was the fact that Hanley was the strongest person she knew. By the same means which he got himself into this jam, he could weave his way out.

Walking to the Greyhound bus station, Eavlyn bobbed through busy businessmen in hot pursuit of their dreams. Up above, she could see the Statue of Liberty. Its posture was straight, its character tall. The statue was meant to be a symbol of freedom in America and it represented having the right to do whatever one pleases without interfering in the next man's life.

In a spur of the moment, Eavlyn wondered what part of the city she was in. Brooklyn, Times Square, or Harlem? Who knew?

Just then, a powerful emotion of getting home rinses her of these thoughts and she is ready to get back to Virginia. The bus stop loomed ahead. It is large, outlandish, and boisterous. Eavlyn can barely read the digital bus numbers.

She watches as pigeons and doves land on the outback of the bus station. The birds remind her of the setup that Hanley's parents owned. They had a beautiful establishment, some acres full. Cattle, oxen, and buffalo ran free. Hanley's father and grandfather lived there now. The two had let the place go since Hanley's mother's death. At least, they had let it go since the last time Eavlyn visited.

Eavlyn felt bad for them. But not that bad. A house full of grown men could take care of themselves. Look at her. She had been abandoned and widowed. Her health stressed. Eavlyn's family had left her to *rot in peace*. However, refusing to R.I.P., she learned self-love, discipline, and individualism. Her strength was tested until she had no choice but to fail. And Eavlyn's soul flourished. Every man for himself. Eavlyn had become a master of the game.

Some wind chimes in the distance made edible music as Eavlyn's hair blew with the wind. When the wind picked up like this on her establishment, the cows she owned ran for cover around the clothesline. Eavlyn adored whenever her cows did this and she'd milk them on the spot since they were already tensed. Eavlyn's motivation of owning cows came from her education on how manufactured milk was made.

Cows were milked by stainless steel machines and then the liquid was sent inside a processor for pasteurization. This is what she despised the most. On her account, pasteurization was not only expendable; it took away vitamins that were essential to the human body. "In Dairy Inc.," a milk education visual, it showed her how dirty manufactured milk got during processing. And to think: this was the very stuff she was born off.

So she raised and bred her own cows. Made sure they had clean food and grass to eat.

Bus 15, her ride, was yards from the bus takeoff. Eavlyn mounted the steps and showed the bus driver her Greyhound bus pass. He accepted it and cast a lustful eye on Eavlyn's chest. With a fresh mouth, the bus driver took a liking to her.

"Eavlyn, eh?" he said with a geechy accent. "So which stop you headed?"

"Lame!" A young man in the seat behind the driver clowns him. Then to Eavlyn the young man said, "Ma'am don't pay Mr. Desperate here any mind."

"Player hater," said the bus driver. "You're just mad 'cause ladies never give a back seat driver any play."

Eavlyn takes her seat on the driver's side, almost at the middle of the bus, smiling. Compliments made her feel good.

She placed all her belongings adjacent, until someone came to fill the seat. Until then she kicked her feet on the safety rest and she enjoyed the scenery as the bus drove off, south. The bus took a dipping turn driving down a hill. Care-free, Eavlyn blew any unwanted stress out as the Greyhound popped diesel through its duel pipes. "Reeu-oomm..."

Powerful was the rumbling's, reminding her of her god-son's episode in the Bank. Being a paper chaser, Hanley will always have his mind on the mucho-dinero. She knew it and he knew it. It was useless to worry about Hanley because a man chasing money is in the proper race. Hanley's motives were excusable.

Reprehensible, Eavlyn closed her eyes. She did the right thing for Hanley and for herself. She opens her eyes, riding out the wave out in this overwhelming ocean. The Greyhound bus seemed small amongst the large structures of the city. To Eavlyn, it was all unreal. Eavlyn kicked her high heels back, relaxed, and bathed in the real life portrait of the mega-sized paintings of a master piece.

MIND MADE UP

—

The wobbling movements from the seesaw made him think of his own childhood. Approaching his twin daughter and son on the playground, he grabbed his keys from his right pocket and gestured toward them. "You people wrapping it up?" Watching his kids bouncing up and down reminded him of how rough he had had it growing up. Boomerang back and forth from foster home, his childhood was interrupted by having to fend for himself at an early age, so he promised he'd nourish his seeds better one day. He took his young-ins somewhere special every first of the month. This month, like last, it was the public playground. Soon they wanted to see Chuck E. Cheese, complaining to their father they've missed Chuck since their last birthday.

In about four months the twins would be starting kindergarten. Their father was working double shifts so they could attend an elite private school. They'd be five when they started school and both parents would be glad when they did.

Mom and dad were T.I.R.E.D. Toddlers: It Ruined Everyone's Drive.

Their mother had breast fed them and worked with them herself. They were ready. Kai was born 50 seconds before baby boy Kurt.

"Come on you two," their father said, wiping sand off

Kurt as he took his hand. They had had played in the sand how they'd do at the beach, making sand castles and shit.

"Kai we're leaving. Do you want to get left?"

"Coming daddy. I have to get my crown from off the mansion top," she said.

To scare her, the father walked to the curb holding Kurt's hand. Kai came running to them from the sand. "Did you get it?" Kurt asked.

"Yep. Daddy why were you rushing me?"

"When I say jump, you say how high," he said. His daughter Kai was like her mother this way, hating to be told what to do. He grabbed her hand with his free hand and walked Kai and Kurt back to the Duplex.

"You people hungry yet?" he asked, settling in his home.

"We just ate," Kai answered. "Daddy put the garage up so we can ride our bikes."

It surprised him how much she had taken from her mother. Kai would not be a kid very long. "Is that right, Kurt?"

Kurt was somewhere in the bathroom, so Kai answered for him. "He said yep. We're ready."

"Well just give me a minute. I need to eat something, myself."

Kai strutted off. "We'll be waiting," she said, ignoring what her father said.

He rubbed over his haircut and went to use his bathroom. When he got out he fixed a roast beef sub. He made a cup of ice water then went in the garage to find the twins both sitting on their bikes.

So daddy let the garage up. "I'll watch you people from the kitchen," he said. "So make sure you guys ride close to the house."

"Will do," Kurt said. "Dad my teeth hurt. They've been hurting since yesterday."

"What have you eaten?"

Kurt thought hard. "I ate that bag of jolly ranchers and chicken. And sum bubble gum today."

"Just wait it out. Probably another snagged tooth ache."

He went back into the house and the kids rolled out of the garage on their bikes. Kurt was on training wheels. Kai could ride without them.

When he got back into the kitchen, he ate his foot long sub as he watched the twins play on their bikes. Sparkling and decorative, he admired himself for picking out those bikes for them last Christmas.

He watched them ride their bikes through the Windex-ed windows. Kurt rode behind Kai. Mannie ate his sub. The glass of water suited the sub in his mouth.

Alone in the house, Mannie suddenly heard a noise from his homemade office. It was a "ding" from his Facebook in-box. Someone had sent him a Facebook posting on his wall! He took a peek out at the twins before he went.

The message was from their mother Alysha. It read: *'Dear Mannie, I should be back home next week. Please don't ask exactly when. I hope Double Duo is doing well. lol '*

Pleased that Alysha is respecting his Facebook communication wish instead of wasting precious minutes by cell phone, Mannie writes her back:

'What sort of things did you get into up there? Or should I say

whose thing got into you? Then Mannie remembered Kurt's teeth. *'Kurt says his teeth are aching. Do you have any idea what may be wrong with them?'*

Alysha took a flight via her job and flew to a hair show. She got to connect with new professionals, experiment with new styles, and make money. Her promiscuous reputation was well known by Mannie, and things got complicated when they could not communicate because he automatically assumed she was lying to him. They were not married or seeing each other.

Within a moment Alysha writes him back. *'I'm responsible Mannie. And Kurt may have a toothache. It could be serious though. He could have a premature cavity. Take him to the dentist. If you don't, I will.'*

He doesn't write her back. Mannie understands she has likely slept with someone while on vacation. Swearing not to talk to her until she comes back, Mannie leaves the computer and heads back to the kitchen to eat.

If Kurt needed a dentist, she would have to take him.

It is this very thing that handicaps their relationship. Alysha goes to cheating, which triggers his act to cheat back. Setting their chances to be together further apart.

Alysha and Mannie had only two kids together. They were sort of in love with each other when the fraternal twins were conceived. They were young and gradually developed "other" interests and begin seeing other people, all while keeping the twins out of there dysfunctional relationship. He moved the twins into his Duplex but Alysha kept seeing people, albeit an attempt at a two parent household.

Watching his kids ride on a driveway across the street, Mannie counts the days until Alysha will come back so he knows when he can stop picking the twins up from Day care. He has two full shifts on Saturday of next week so he will not be able to pick them up then.

Six days, he counts.

Through the kitchen window, an elderly man wearing a headband walks towards the twins. Mannie has seen this man out exercising before. The elderly man stops and chumps it up with the twins. Mannie watches suspiciously.

"Bastard's a Child Predator!"

No sir. Mannie dashes to the door, opening it to find the elderly man jogging off and the twins racing around each other in circles.

Mannie wouldn't risk it. "Kai, Kurt! I want you inside now! The sky looks tempting."

He finishes his All World Sub then goes back into the garage, shuts and locks it after the twins have come in.

He goes back to his office and navigates to *Geico.com*. He reads and studies the Customer Insurance Policy page. A few days ago he received an e-mail from Geico Insurance saying that insurance on his only vehicle would be going up by 75 bucks. Already hurt by this, a FedEx delivery package came in the mail confirming this situation. All this was due to the twins starting school. His insurance company thought he'd be transporting them in his Gran Torino, of which Ford no longer made, and the risk factor rose. Geico didn't understand that a bus from the private school would be picking the twins up.

Next to his office was the living room. The twins were now in it. Kurt yelled, "Dad, where are you?"

Kai said: "Hush Boy! And flip to *Keeping up with the Kardashian's*."

Mannie has been writing Geico every day now. Paying

for his car insurance was hard. A raise on his 1972 Gran
Torino would be like a shot in the veins. Sending his Geico assistant an e-mail, explaining the whole situation with
his car, he turned the computer off.

"Did I hear someone say DAD?" he said to the twins,
beating on his chest.

"Yes," Kurt said. "I'm hungry again."

Mannie grabbed Kurt and flipped him up into the air.
"Let's fill your belly button up with that air pump over
there. If you say one more thing, it's over! I'll destroy you!
"

The twins were a handful and though he had
problems of his own, the twins were simply too much fun.
To the 2nd Power!

———

Hustling fresh towels over to the Nurse and Doctor
Sweet, Mannie ejected out orders like he was a drill sergeant. "If I put a red beam on your foreheads would that
make you zombie's move faster?"

Mannie cursed all workers in general. The workers
were used to this motivation talk, especially after the
weekend had concluded and they were less energetic.

Mannie was always energetic. A week went by and
Alysha told him she had the kids covered after Day care.
He saluted her. And then apologized for not taking Kurt
to the dentist.

Alysha scolded him for this. "You couldn't what?"
She got on his ass. She yelled and raged that he was a los-
er. Why? All because she didn't want to pay for Kurt's
check-up. Especially considering the twins didn't have

health insurance.

"Cavities turn into root canals if you don't get them filled! Root canal's cost $1 thousand dollars! I had a root canal growing up and I couldn't afford getting it fixed! So they had to pull one of my teeth instead!"

Mannie entered Doctor DueHart's office sweet. Mannie needed to ask him if he knew a Dentist that did checkups and dental work for cheap. He spotted Dr. DueHart's bent over, sifting through cabinets trying to find whatever. Refusing to greet his personal arch rival, Mannie laid the towels on the shelf—being aggravating on purpose.

"Who's there?" asked DueHart, turning around.

"The dog with no ears," he said.

DueHart giggled. "It doesn't matter what I call you because I can't hear you."

"Impressive," said Mannie reassuringly. "Most people don't get that joke. Anyways, I have a question for you. My son teeth are hurting him—I wonder if you knew a cheap Dentist to could recommend him?"

"Let's see, *cheap dentist*...I'm sorry Mannie. I'm not associated with any Dentists. At all."

Bravo. Mannie found this hard to believe. "Then who is your Dentist, Doc?" he wanted to ask.

"Doctor DueHart. What sort of doctor are you anyway?"

"A Dermatologist."

"Sure." Mannie zoomed out the room, the towels left lying patient on the sink.

Doctor DueHart and Mannie went to the same church and saw each other every other Sunday. Mannie was a hater of the young doctor and DueHart knew it. The past weekend DueHart went to Niagara Falls. Next week would be the 15 of the month and he was planning to order a passport to Australia to see Tropical Forests for the first time.

Dr. DueHart moved liked the president.

On Sundays, DueHart paid his tithes at Orlando Faith Ministries every week but sometimes couldn't make it home in time. Orlando Faith was a big church that hosted spiritual events on a daily basis for the community and for its faithful members. Located in the downtown of Orlando, it represented the concentration of adults in their prime, active and "making moves." The the pastor was 25.

Back to work, Mannie made sure everyone under management was caught up in the swing of things. When he was certain, he made his way to the bottom floor and punched out. The time was 11:30 at night.

When Mannie got home, a message from Geico said that he would have to show proof that his kids would be bus pooled. He stomped hard with his dress shoes: proof?

He writes a message back saying how long that would take. In the letter he uses nasty words, threatening to find a less expensive Insurance Company with lower rates.

Almost a week passes by when he comes to the Duplex and finds a message from Alysha. *Kurt had two cavities and I got them filled for $155.*

Mannie is relieved. He writes back. *Where are the twins staying?*

At my parents.

Fully relieved now, Mannie writes back: *Why won't you and the twins live with me. I'm getting lonely.*

She doesn't write back and Mannie doesn't expect her

to. He goes and prepares a bowl of Roman Noodles for himself. Adding some fresh Cajun shrimp to the dish.

Rolling into the third week of the month, Mannie is on his A-Game at work, deciding to strive for his best which always makes everyone around him try harder. When he leaves work he logs onto to Sharebuilder.com to check his stocks. He is a stock owner with two elementary bonds for Starbucks, originally bought for two Andrew Jackson dollar bills. Both stocks are now worth 50 dollars.

He would sell the stocks for a gain, of course. Eventually.

Elsewhere, Alysha was supposed to bring the twins around to see their father this Friday. Mannie suggested her to spend the night herself, hoping to trap her into staying.

On Tuesday the Duplex door is cracked open at 7:00 as Mannie comes home from his first shift. Home to dream for a few hours. That's all he could do. Dream life would be better tomorrow.

Alysha is sitting on the swede couches under a small lamp next to his office. She greets him.

"I see your car insurance will be going up?"

"Yes." Mannie says, placing grocery bags on the kitchen counter. "Where are the twins?" he said, walking to where Alysha is sitting.

"Sleep."

"Well glad you made this decision." He went and sat beside her. "I've missed you. What have you been up to? The twins are a handful, huh."

"No, the twins are good—"

Mannie interrupts. "Speak for yourself."

"I've been running the Hair Salon a lot lately with my

manager out," Alysha confesses. "We have a hair show next month. I was one of the beauticians nominated to go."

"Cool. You touring everywhere and stuff. Just make sure you spend quality time with the kids. They're not getting any younger. Kai is going on fifteen." He scooted closer toward Alysha.

"Girls grow up faster than boys," she said. "Don't you have to go to work later today?"

"Yes at ten."

Alysha asked for his job phone number.

"Excuse me Mannie," she said answering a call. She said "Hello," and talked to someone named DueHart and told them Mannie would not be able to come in today.

"There," she says.

"What was that for? I can't work just because you're here?"

"Yes, Mannie," Alysha explained. "With me making the cash like I'm making at the Salon, you won't have to do double shifts. I'm sure I can pay the difference for the twin's school costs."

He looked deep into her eyes and caked one of her twists in his fingers.

"Boy you fucking up my weave!"

"Oh, sorry. I just don't know what to say."

"If you don't mind, the twins like it here. I was wondering if I paid you 300 a month could I stay here too?"

"Yes!" Mannie always had love for his baby momma. "Damn. Who says you can't have your cake and eat it?"

"Hush boy. You'll wake the twins up. Deal?"

"Signed and Stamped."

Mannie is elated that Alysha wants to be a family

again. He will make the most of this chance. Forever trying to make a dish, the self-starter in Mannie announces
that he will make Hamburger Helper for dinner to cele-
brate. "You will like how I make my Helper."

"I already ordered pizza. Papa Johns if you want to
know."

Mannie looked sad. "Word? Well then carry on." He
scoots closer to her. "Say Alysha, what have you been doing these past few weeks. I'll tell you what I've been up to:
I haven't been sexing anyone."

"Mannie you 'wanna know the truth? In New Orleans
a guy brought me to his condo and sat me down and
dined me, candle lights, wine, the whole nine. We talked,
he kept drinking, and then before you know it, he took me
to the bed and pasted out dread on it. We did nothing. I
was disappointed 'cause I forgot my toothbrush and had
to buy one. As far as the pass few weeks, I've been working nonstop at the shop like I told you. No days off."

Mannie breathed a deep sigh of relief. "Thank God. I
thought I loosed you. I mean with you doing all that traveling and stuff, I was afraid someone might scoop you up.
I'm thankful for this second chance, if I can call it that."

"Don't call it that. You're doing me the favor." She
smiled and they hugged for a long while. Mannie was de-
termined to keep her.

Alysha gingerly gripped his head with each hand and
pats it. "I didn't realize you had so many gray hairs," she
noted.

Mannie had a lot of gray strands, plus he had more to
grow. He worked hard and he would have to work harder
now that he had a family. He was ready. Family completed
him. He knew it. Young man, old man mind.

Mannie and Alysha embraced a long kiss as they fell into each others arms. The Duplex grew silent, just the two lovebirds rekindling their fire for each other.

Outside, the pizza man knocked on the door with all his might. "Knock, Knock!" He glanced at his lime green G-Shock that glowed in the dark. "Papa Johns!"

—

Orlando Faith Ministries was super charged today, the Holy Ghost live this Sunday which happened to be the last day of the month. Almost all one thousand seats are filled and the choir sings at the top of its lung to drown out the members getting seated by ushers.

"Hallelujah Jesus! Dear God we give you Praise!"

It is a full house. The important ministers and members of the Church sit in the front with the preacher's wife. The pulpit is at the front of the stage, separating the massive choir.

The carpeting for the service is velvet underneath the honey nut benches. Along the perimeter, peach walls adorn the sides on up to the ceiling. Gargantuan chandeliers are spaced apart, hung in the air above speakers and cameras. Fake plants around the stage give the service a jungle feel as the ushers carry out their heavenly missions and orchestrate church goers into seats.

When the pastor stepped up to the pulpit, the noise dimmed down and camera men took their positions. The pastor was clean cut and his suit sharp. "Amen," he said, intercepting the choir's lead. He paused for dramatic effect.

"Thank God for another Sunday," he said with his islander accent. "Amen! Can I get an 'Amen' church?"

"Amen!" The church body shouted back and then naturally became quiet.

"You know as I was home with my wife yesterday night, I became nostalgic of the Earth beauty we have taken for granted. And it dawned upon me how much we 'already have without money. How much we have without secular things money can buy. How much we have before we look over our shoulders at our neighbors."

A baby burst out crying as a mother hurried for the bathroom to pacify her little one.

The pastor took a sip of water. Born in Jamaica, he was some story in that he was a former Rastafarian who converted to Christianity when he came to America. Fresh off the boat. Finding himself in a blessed religion, he cut off his long dreadlocks and became a believer of the Christian church.

"When people get money 'does there perception 'change. Their attitude, there appetite. Uh, Can I get a witness! Money makes people's health change. Don't feel sorry. We're all victims of 'eet. People get caught up in 'sumthing that is made from man! Man! Not God, but Man! But the things made by god remain most 'natural and beautiful things we have on 'dis Planet! The Sun, the Beech, Trees, Sky! The Moon! Amen! Conformation to the world is what makes us blinded by 'worldly things! Bogus that has Notheen to do with Jesus Christ! For the bible says what? Be not conformed to the world, but transformed by the renewing of your mind! People, 'Money is the Root of All Evil!"

"Amen! Amen!" The church service agreed in accordance.

Way back in the left row, Mannie sat on the end of the isle, clapping beside Alysha. The twins came and the Sunday school instructor collected them .

"Come on now Pastor!"

Out of the corner of Mannie's eye, an iota of red snapped him into turning around. What he saw made him almost fall out of his seat. Doctor DueHart was sharply dressed in a lavish Lamborghini red tuxedo, with a diamond tie glittering up at the church. Cameo Appearance.

Take A Picture.

His flow shiners are pink and they match the dress of that bad bitch on his arm. Mannie assumes she is his girlfriend. When DueHart passes by, he winks at Mannie who nods back in approval. Accepting his champion, his ego.

The Doctor's money was on another level.

Alysha bumped Mannie. "What was that all about?"

"Life baby. Life."

Church comes to a conclusion and Mannie rounds up his family, telling the twins where he is taking them tomorrow: The Church again for some baptizing. Mannie even convinces Alysha to join them.

Orlando was always one of his favorite places to visit. Living in Melbourne, Mannie seldom got to see the city like he wanted to.

Ready for the road, the church family held hands as a final prayer released everyone.

Caught in the moment, he prays to do whatever to keep his family together. He was raised in a two parent household and it would be selfish not to give the same to his seeds.

With Alysha splitting rent, he vows to send extra cash into his savings account. Starting with the most important issue at hand: Car Insurance.

AUTHOR ACKNOWLEDGMENTS

I write. It is something I always loved to do. I remember being a kid and scribbling led onto paper then balling them into the trash. Writing was fun. So I stuck with it. And people thought I was good. With that, allow me to thank those who helped me make it this far. First place thanks goes to Monica Davis. Dear Mama, you initiated my love for reading and writing. I remember sitting in your room and reading to you. You gave me options. And I thank you for that.

Let me give thanks to family and friends who ever gave me feedback on my stories. This motivated me to continue improving. My publisher also played a role by recognizing my work and taking a chance on a new writer. I appreciate your faith. Last but not least, I thank God for blessing me with such gifts. I love to write and God gave me the chance to show the world what I can do.

Contact Cameron at:
- www.twitter.com/daviscis1 (website)
- cameron5@mail.usf.edu (email)